LOVING MEMORY

Gerald Hammond titles available from Severn House Large Print

LOVING MEMORY

Gerald Hammond

Severn House Large Print
London & New York

This first large print edition published 2008
in Great Britain and the USA by
SEVERN HOUSE PUBLISHERS of
9-15 High Street, Sutton, Surrey, SM1 1DF.
First world regular print edition published 2007 by
Severn House Publishers, London and New York.

British Library Cataloguing in Publication Data

Hammond, Gerald, 1926-
  Loving memory. - Large print ed.
  1. Women detectives - Scotland - Fiction 2. Detective and
  mystery stories 3. Large type books
  I. Title
  823.9'14[F]

  ISBN-13: 978-0-7278-7726-0

Printed and bound in Great Britain by
MPG Books Ltd, Bodmin, Cornwall

One

Mr Potterton-Phipps was on the phone to his daughter. 'I'm thinking of changing the Range Rover,' he said.

'Again?'

'Yes. I made a mistake accepting part-fabric seats instead of all leather and I hate the colour now that I see it full size and in daylight. There are one or two other things. So, if you'd like to let me have its predecessor back to trade in, Honeypot, you can have this one in exchange. It's hardly even run in.'

Detective Inspector Laird had been born Honoria Potterton-Phipps and she had grown from an attractive baby into an equally attractive woman, though she herself was rarely aware of it. During her salad days, men were drawn to her. It was therefore inevitable that she would be known as Honeypot and the nickname had stuck. She was still trying to live it down, preferring to be addressed by family and intimates as Honey, and it was a source of satisfaction to her that her father sometimes remembered that she disliked its use. 'Thank you kindly, Dad,' she said. The black Labrador by her feet emitted a loud snore and received a push from Honey's slipper. 'But I've just got everything in this one the way I want it and it's not very much more than run in. You trade that one in and perhaps in another couple of years we'll think about another swap.'

'So be it. My regards to Sandy and love to the Mighty Midget. Bye, Honeypot.' He hung up quickly before his daughter could find a suitable retort.

Chief Inspector Alexander 'Sandy' Laird was nursing his month-old daughter and looking surprisingly at home in the act. Honey explained the burden of her conversation with her father and Sandy tried not to sigh aloud. It was an effort that he had had to make more than once in the past. Most men might consider themselves lucky to marry the attractive only daughter of a major landowner, one who was also a captain of industry. Sandy, however, usually resented his wife's affluence and made a show of standing on his own feet. But now and again he felt that he just might abandon his Calvinist principles if his father-in-law were to make him such an offer. Mr Potterton-Phipps was in the habit of buying his cars at the very top of what was already an expensive range and then putting them into the hands of specialists for further improvement while Sandy, thanks to his own insistence on paying his share of a quite unnecessary mortgage out of a chief inspector's salary, would have been quite happy with the lesser products of Messrs Ford or Vauxhall were it not for the larger and more opulent vehicle parked beside his. He made a show of being, if not quite the boss, at least the equal in his own home, but he did sometimes feel that his wife might make the effort, just once, to overrule him.

At this point in his ruminations he glanced out into the gloomy Edinburgh street, where the yellow lights were reflecting on the wet surface, and he stiffened. 'I think I'll take Pippa for a walk,' he said. At his words the black Labrador woke instantly and jumped to her feet.

Honeypot recognized the signs. Sandy was not usually a devotee of walking for walking's sake. 'Who's arriving?' she asked.

Sandy decided that honesty was the best policy. Honey could usually see through him. 'It's your friend, Kate Ingliston.'

The elegant room was looking its best with the firelight flickering across the deep carpet and the subdued wall lights adding to the warm glow. It was the kind of cosy scene that one looks forward to in a winter's daytime. It would have taken an effort to turn out into the cold and dusk but Honey muttered, 'I've half a mind to come with you.' She then said more loudly, 'All right then. Hand me the Mighty Midget, let Kate in and then be off with you. Just don't let Pippa roll in anything that you wouldn't roll in yourself or you can shower her in the back garden. And don't let her eat anything too awful or she'll fart all evening.'

'Hang a towel in a back window when she's gone.'

Honey accepted her daughter Minka into her arms, which gave her an excuse not to rise when Sandy showed Kate in and made his escape.

Kate Ingliston should have been past her sexual peak but she managed to remain at or very close to it by a regime of diets, beauty treatments, hormone therapy and swinging weekends. She was well aware that Honey and her husband were strictly monogamous but she was equally aware that Honey was seldom if ever shocked. It was her habit to describe her ventures into wife-swapping (or being swapped) in pleasurable detail, thus prolonging the exquisite naughtiness and helping to fix the details in her own memory. This, Honey supposed, was the reason for the present visit late on a Sunday afternoon.

But apparently not. Kate was not looking her cheerful self and she lacked the sparkle that usually came with her when she was preparing to gloat. After a quick peck on the cheek and a perfunctory enquiry after the baby's progress, Kate said, 'Honey, I need your help. Desperately.'

There was only one emergency that Honey could envisage causing such a stir. 'Black-mail?' she enquired.

Kate's curls were usually tight and firmly positioned. But today they were flying loose, giving her rather the look of a distressed cockatoo, but at Honey's question it looked as though they might stand on end. 'Oh God no! I hope not. Not yet, anyway.'

'You'd better explain. But first, would you like a drink?'

Kate paused. 'God, could I use a drink!' she said. She sounded surprised.

'Help yourself. You could pour me a little one from the decanter.'

'I thought you were still feeding Minka.'

'I am. But it's a very much diluted wine and I only sip until the last feed. It does make sure that she sleeps like a log.' Honey accepted a small glass of diluted claret. 'Now, tell me...'

Kate was speaking before she had completed the act of seating herself. She had a loud voice with a metallic tone. Honey sometimes wondered how she had come to be friendly with anyone who made so much use of such a voice, and would then remember that the friendship was of Kate's making. 'Honey, it's bad. I've had a boyfriend.'

'I noticed the car. I thought your husband must have traded his Audi in.'

'Phil's abroad all this month, setting up something in Malaysia. He won't be back until Wednesday. He'll hit the ceiling if he finds out.'

'This I do not understand,' Honey said. 'The two of you go away on swingers' weekends...'

Kate made a dismissive gesture. 'That's all very well, and quite acceptable if we're both doing it. He'd be furious if I went off on my own. And I must say I can understand that, because I wouldn't like it if I knew that he was having it off with some other woman behind my back. If we both go off at the same time with somebody we know, that's just a giggle and something we can laugh over between ourselves. But for one of us to go off on our own, that's different. You see, then it might be serious,' she said earnestly. 'But it isn't, for me. It's just a piece of fun and a reminder that the days of courtship and glamour and romance are not dead and gone. So he never slept here. We went to a hotel. That's where I was most of the weekend, a week ago.

'On that Sunday, I said a permanent farewell to him. Today, I went golfing with Sandra and Ivy – I don't think you know them – and when I got home the house had been broken into. They cleaned us out of booze and loose cash – not very much, luckily – and some quite expensive odds and ends. My jewellery's gone, but I never had very much and mostly it was small and rubbishy bits, the way it happens when it's been collected over a long period. With a bit of luck,' Kate said thoughtfully, 'the insurance money may provide for fewer but better, which would be a big step up. But Phil's camera was taken.'

'Expensive?' Honey asked. The baby in her arms roused, burped gently and then responded to a little friendly jogging and subsided into sleep again.

'Very! But that isn't the point. All our things are insured.'

'And the camera isn't?' Honey was still groping for the reason behind Kate's obvious agitation.

'It's insured all right. That isn't the problem either. But ... my friend and I used the camera, the way one does –' she looked enquiringly at Honey but received no encouragement – 'on timer delay to ... to...'

The penny dropped at last. 'You mean,'

Honey said bluntly, 'that you used your husband's camera to take photographs of yourself and your lover *in flagrante delicto*?' She tried to keep disapproval out of her voice, but Kate had always seemed to her to be an unattractive figure, having a pointed nose and a figure that was too skinny to be erotic and too angular to be a model. The idea of photographs of that body in raptures with a stranger was disturbing. Honey had been a bit of a girl in her day; she had enjoyed her youth and freedom. If she had been asked now how many lovers had figured in her past, she could only have given an approximate number. But since her marriage to Sandy she had stopped straying and then stopped looking, until now the idea of lingering in any arms but his was unthinkable.

Just as unthinkable to Kate was the concept of so much fidelity. 'Yes. It makes a good turn-on for next time. You must know that, surely?'

Honey ignored the question. 'And the camera has now been stolen?'

'Yes. I looked for it to wipe off the amorous bits before Phil gets home. It's so easy with a digital; it could have been made for that sort of thing. Anyway, it was gone.'

'Have you told the police about your burglary?'

'I'm telling you now. I was waiting for Phil

12

to get home. He deals with all that sort of thing.'

'For the love of Pete,' Honey said impatiently, 'you've got to make a formal report immediately. Otherwise the insurers won't look at any of your claim. You may already be too late.'

'Yes, but I came to you first because I thought you might be able to help.' Kate said this earnestly, as if to a child.

Honey found the idea that she might be able to conjure a stolen camera back from the thief showed a touching faith but she decided to make an effort. 'Was the camera identifiable as yours and Phil's?'

Kate nodded sadly. 'I'm afraid so, or else I'd just have let the burglar keep it and snigger over the pictures. But Phil's very careful about possessions. He has our postcode in UV ink all over things, but he also put one of those stickers on it with our name and address, the ones you get free with charitable appeals.'

'So what you want from me is to get the camera back without anyone seeing the pictures in the memory card?'

Kate made a gesture of helplessness and knocked over her generous drink, which was still at least half full. Honey smelled gin and more gin. 'I don't give a tinker's turd about the camera,' Kate said. 'If I could be sure that it will never surface, I'd be a happy bunny. I'm just hoping that if it does turn up you can get the memory card out of it before some coarse copper gets a look at it and decides to circulate the pictures around his friends – or sell them to a porno magazine.'

Honey was not more than normally house-proud, but the table was a genuine antique and June, the housekeeper, would go berserk if the polish that she had lovingly burnished were to be spoiled. 'If you want my help, go and fetch a damp cloth from the kitchen,' she said. 'My feet are tired, I'm weighed down by baby and you're looking for a favour.'

'Couldn't June...?'

'It's June's night off. And every minute wasted increases the chances of the polish being spoiled and the camera getting away from us.'

In her own house, Kate would have scampered to prevent damage to the furniture, but her principles would have prevented her from doing manual work in somebody else's house. However, she rose reluctantly and left the room, returning with two cloths, one damp and one dry.

When the damage was halted to her satisfaction, Honey said, 'That'll do. June can give it a dab of wax tomorrow. Help yourself to a refill while I phone in. And as far as the police are concerned, you don't know whether Phil had his camera away with him or not.'

'But suppose it does turn up?'

'Then you'll be a liar as well as a trollop. Would that be so very much worse? No, don't wave your arms around or you'll spill more gin and I'll have to have the table repolished and send you the bill. Would you rather have every copper in the Lothians hunting for a camera with your husband's name on it and your pictures inside?'

'I see what you mean,' Kate said. She poured more gin thoughtfully.

Honey phoned the control room. There is a lassitude that comes over police buildings late on a Sunday when the few staff on duty resent the fact that the others are out on the town and can be pictured, sometimes wrongly, drinking or participating in orgies. Even for Detective Inspector Laird, no officers were likely to be available for several hours.

'I believe that there were guns in the house,' Honey said. That, apparently, was different.

'There's a car on the way.'

'Tell them to come to my house, just across the street and a little way up the hill.' She disconnected.

Kate was looking at her as though she had

lost her marbles. 'There aren't any guns in my house. There never were.'

'If you think back, you'll realize that I never said that there were. Are you prepared to offer a reward for the camera?'

'I suppose so. A hundred?'

'That might do it. It's about the second-hand value of a miniature digital. But it does seem rather miserable when you set it against the risk ... er ... were you in the nude?'

'Worse.'

'Well, then. Imagine that image being passed around or exchanged on the Internet.'

'Two hundred and fifty, then,' Kate said. 'And I'll pay that just for the memory card if I have to.'

'That's more like it.'

Two CID officers, a sergeant and a constable both known to Honey, arrived in an unmarked car and in a remarkably short time. Kate brought them into the sitting room.

'Mrs Ingliston's house was broken into,' Honey said. 'I've been telling her that she should have reported it as soon as she discovered it, so there's no need to smack her wrist again. Please go with her and do the usual. I'd come with you except that, as you can see, my hands are rather full. Oh, and a word of apology,' she said as an apparent afterthought. 'I said that I thought there had been guns in the house, but it seems that my memory was at fault and I was acting on the recollection of a couple of toy guns that I had seen in her house some time ago.'

The two officers said that they quite understood. Honey could see that they understood such aberrations to be normal in their seniors in CID.

Carrying her baby with care, Honey got up and set off up the stairs. She fetched a towel from the warm, clean-smelling airing cupboard to put in the window of the upstairs bathroom. Sandy would be walking by moonlight on the farmland that the house backed on to. He would probably be lurking, waiting for the signal, but in case he was out of sight for the moment she left the light on.

Two

'You didn't eat more than a bittie of the dinner I left for you,' June grumbled. 'You need to build up while you're eating for two.'

Honey was also feeding for two at the kitchen table, suckling Minka while taking her own breakfast cereal at the kitchen table. Breakfast was the only time of day when she was allowed to undertake anything useful in the kitchen without provoking a hurricane of sighs and groans from June.

'I'm only a middleman around here,' Honey said. 'Or is *middleperson* a word? Mr Sandy had eaten at the golf club before he came home and I'm trying to shake off the extra weight.'

'You're thin as a rake already,' June retorted.

'I wish. I'm supposed to be on maternity leave to get fit again. Anyway, my milk's getting less and her appetite's getting more. You'd better warm a bottle. Mrs Ingliston will be phoning or coming over soon. If she phones, bring me the cordless. If she comes, bring her into the sitting room and you can take over Minka for me.'

June brightened. She had come to the Laird household as cook and housekeeper – the two functions that her mother carried out for Honey's father – but her favourite duties by far were as nursemaid and nanny. June's mother was beginning to find the work of running Mr Potterton-Phipp's household to be hard work for one of her years and her employer had started dropping hints that perhaps it was time that she retired and that June came back to take over, a suggestion that was opposed by June's present employers and no less by June herself, with many mentions of dead bodies and other obstacles that would first have to be overcome.

When the supply of Honeymilk ran out that morning, young Miss Laird made it clear that she was by no means satisfied. Honey was happy to deliver her to June for topping-up from the feeding bottle while she herself retired upstairs. Honey was in the shower when she heard the doorbell. Coming downstairs ten minutes later she found Kate in the kitchen, restored to her usual immaculate state and nursing an already somnolent Minka while June washed up. Once burped, the baby settled down contentedly under June's eye and the two ladies adjourned to the sitting room. The room was comfortably warm from the central heating but the imitation coal portion of an electric appliance, placed in front of the dead ashes of the previous evening, conveyed a spurious impression of an open fire.

'How did you get on?' Honey asked.

'They're thorough, I'll say that for them. When they left it was after midnight. I looked across but there were no lights on here and there didn't seem to be much point disturbing you. I made them sandwiches, which was all they'd take. They looked at the window the thieves had jemmied to get in and they tried every possible surface for fingerprints. Of course they found about ten thousand fingerprints but those that aren't mine will turn out to belong to Phil or my cleaning lady. I gave them details of the camera. I said that my husband might have it with him but that we'd be very upset if it was gone for good because it held photographs of an occasion that had great sentimental value and could never be repeated. Don't laugh, it was almost true. What happens next?'

'In an ideal world,' Honey said, 'the entire CID would be dashing around, shaking down every known fence or tealeaf and looking out for anything on your stolen list. In this less than perfect world there simply isn't time for that sort of concentration on every break-in. Unless somebody was killed, of course. You didn't have the foresight to lure a stranger into your home and brain them with the poker?'

'Never thought of it.'

'A mistake. Your chattels would have become clues. You'd have had everybody looking for them instead of waiting for some of them to surface if a thief or a fence comes a cropper. You've notified your insurers?'

'I phoned. They're sending an adjuster.'

'Stay vague about the camera. Meanwhile, I'll see what I can do.'

Kate's face drooped with depression and her voice, usually penetrating to the point at which Honey had to make a conscious effort not to flinch, had dropped to a level at which Honey found it quite tolerable. 'Honey, you're not cheering me up much,' she said. 'I can't see you dashing around, intimidating – what do you call them? – snouts. Not with a young babe in arms.'

Honey laughed. Hearing her own laugh always surprised her with its warmth and richness. 'You watch too much TV,' she said. 'I don't need to dash about. What do you think is the investigator's principal tool?'

Kate looked vague. Evidently she had never paused to consider how the police might do their job. 'I don't know. Fingerprint kit?'

'Telephone,' Honey said. 'Backed up by fax and email. I have an informant – I suppose you'd call him a snout. He knows most of what's going on. After you left here last night I phoned him, gave him the details and mentioned the reward. I don't know that he can find your camera but I know that he'll try.'

Kate reached for the handbag beside her chair. 'Do you pay him?'

'Keep your filthy lucre. No. In a sense, I paid him long ago. In those days he had a junk shop and wasn't too fussy about what he bought or sold. I'd have run him in like a shot and he knew it. Then a dishonest policeman – you'd probably call him a bent copper – got hold of him and tried to shake him down for money by threatening his daughter with prosecution as a street-walker. I knew the girl and I knew that she wasn't any such thing. To cut a long story very short, I got it dropped and the copper was given the push. Her father can't do enough for me. He has two antique shops now and he'll buy and sell absolutely anything. I'll still run him in if he slips up, but until that day he's a heaven-sent source of information.'

'What an exciting life you lead!' Kate glanced at her watch. 'I have to go soon. The insurance man will be coming and then I've got my cleaning lady. She'll help me to put everything back together again.'

'You can manage a coffee before you go?'

They had coffee. When Kate rose, Honey escorted her to the door. There was some mail on the doormat. There was also a large, padded envelope with neither address nor stamps on it. Honey opened this first. It contained a Nikon camera. She held it out. Kate grabbed it and slid the little door so that it sprang open. Together they looked inside.

'The memory card's been taken out,' Kate said. Suddenly, she looked ten years older.

'It held the only copies?'

Kate looked puzzled. 'I don't get you.'

In Honey's line of work it soon became habitual to think all round a situation. She had come to expect her colleagues to follow her trains of thought. 'Neither you nor your friend,' Honey said patiently, 'had downloaded the contents of the memory card into a computer to store it or view it or to make prints, in order to wind yourselves up again? Because, if so, your happy snaps will also be in the computer's memory and that's another set to worry about.'

'No, nothing like that, thank God. We had a quick scroll through, looking at them on the camera's little screen, and that was all that we—'

'Let's take the details as read, shall we?'

23

Honey said firmly. After dalliance with a much loved husband at bedtime the previous evening she preferred to keep her memories pristine and not sullied with images of Kate and a stranger who was becoming more and more weird in her imagination. 'So we have to concentrate on the memory card. If I understand digital photography correctly, the camera has no memory of its own and with the memory card or memory stick removed you can safely return his camera to your still loving husband. Does he know yet that you've been burgled?'

Dumbly, Kate shook her head. 'I haven't spoken to him again.'

'Tell him as soon as you can. You'd better leave the rest of the problem with me,' Honey said. 'Keep the camera. Buy another memory card for it. Take a few photographs on it. Tell Phil about the burglary.'

'Shall I tell him that I had the camera with me?'

'If you can be quite sure that he'll never discuss the crime with your cops. After that, you can go on listing everything you can think of that's gone walkies while I make use of my favourite investigatory tool.'

Rather than keep Honey back from her telephoning, Kate was in a hurry to escape. The return of the camera without the memory card had caused her to look more rather than less miserable. Honey saw her to the door and took a look at the weather. The day, which had started damp, had turned bright and clear. She looked into the kitchen. It was the habit of Mr Potterton-Phipps, at the first mention of missed periods or morning sickness, to heap gifts on whichever daughter-in-law was expecting his grandchild and Honey's sisters-in-law, once they were quite sure that their childbearing days were over, had passed on to Honey much expensive baby gear. This had included several cots, which made it possible to have one in each room so that Minka could be put down to sleep in almost any room without the bother of moving cots around. Minka was sleeping soundly in one that always sat, out of the way of all draughts, between the cooker and the big dresser. June was finishing the washing up.

'I have some phoning to do,' Honey said. 'But Pippa will need a walk. You can leave Minka with me and walk the dog.'

June started to dry her hands hastily. 'She won't get much sleep if you're talking on the phone. I can take the pram and keep Pippa on the lead until we're away from traffic. We'll go up the farm track. The beds can wait until I come back.'

Honey smiled secretly. This had been her intention all along, but she could not have suggested it without enduring an interminable complaint, which would have included a summary of how many pairs of hands June had been blessed with.

Three

As soon as Honey had the house to herself she phoned her informant. Mr Briar had left home and was not to be found at either of his shops. She left urgent messages and eventually he called her back as she had known he would. He was one of the few people who could be trusted to return a call.

'You got the camera?' he asked.

'I did, and I'm deeply grateful. I would have been several times more grateful if the memory card had still been in it. There was some confidential material in the card that my friend would not want to fall into other hands.'

She heard his indrawn breath. 'I don't know about that, Mrs Laird. I'm a jeweller, no' a photographer.'

'You're a...' She hesitated long enough between choosing the words *crook* and *fence* that discretion had time to prevail. ' ... a great help,' she substituted. 'Was the card still in the camera when it left your hands? I take it that it did leave your hands?'

27

'Oh aye.' Though he had lived in Edinburgh for forty years there were traces of his rural origin in Mr Briar's voice. 'It was a part-exchange. Whether there was still a card in it I would not know.'

Honey made a horrible face at the wall. This did not look good. The camera could have changed hands as part of the price of some hot goods. With a modern digital camera it was easy to inspect the photographs still in the memory card or stick given a computer and also a programme, at least one example of which was obtainable free over the Internet. Or else they could be viewed on the camera's screen though to a tiny scale. The memory card might have been viewed and stolen by an employee in Mr Briar's shop, or even a prospective customer, or it might have been traded with the camera and discovered by the purchaser. 'This is important,' she said. 'Can you find out from your staff whether the card was in place when the camera was traded. Who did you pass it on to?'

She did not expect him to name names so she was not disappointed. 'Leave it with me, Mrs Laird,' he said. 'I'll do all that can be done.'

'Please do.' The message seemed to be in need of ramming home. 'This is no longer a matter of getting a favour from an old friend.

If my friend and neighbour suffers blackmail over what's in that camera or if that material gets out in any other way, I shall be very angry indeed. Have you ever seen me really angry, Mr Briar?'

She heard his swift intake of breath. She could see him as clearly as if he had been in front of her – fat and pasty in a too-tight suit that had acquired a shine over the years. 'As it happens, Mrs Laird, I have. Like when Rory Mac tried to kill a witness you were protecting. And when two tykes on day release from Saughton beat up a tart to rob her. You put the fear of God into them, the fuzz, the probationary staff and the psychiatric service. I'm told that when the parole board heard that you were coming to address them, they went and hid in the lavatories.'

'That story,' Honey said, 'was greatly exaggerated. But please believe, if it had been true, my wrath if those pictures ever get public will make that incident look like a childish tantrum.'

'Please, Mrs Laird, leave it in my hands.'

Honey rather thought that she was not getting the run-around but there would be no harm rubbing the message a little further in. 'Your staff have handled stolen goods. There may be a very serious outcome. You've heard the expression "heads will roll"?' she enquired grimly. 'Heads will not merely roll. They will bounce, bungee jump and explode on hitting the ground. If you don't want your head to be one of them, *get that bloody memory card back for me.*'

She disconnected, wondering why she was taking so much trouble and expending favours that could have been used on worthier causes.

For two days, Honey heard nothing except for the plaintive telephoning of Kate Ingliston. At first she had withheld the bad news. Why make Kate miserable when it could serve no good purpose and all might yet be well? Eventually she could no longer defer making a progress report. The only comfort that she could offer to Kate was that no news was, for the moment, good news. Quite possibly the new owner of the memory card had discovered Kate's photographs but was quite unaware of the identity of the subjects and was retaining the photographs for his own delectation and the amusement of his (or her) friends. Kate could only hope that those friends did not include any of her own acquaintances. Even so, it was not a comforting subject for thought.

Phil had returned home but, in accordance with Honey's suggestion, Kate had bought a new memory card to replace the stolen one and embellished it with the postcode. She had then taken several perfectly innocuous photographs of the neighbourhood. Phil was now happily recording his visits to industrial installations in Scotland. Before leaving for his foreign tour he had spent an afternoon printing his recent photographs and transferring to disc the images of any that he wished to preserve. Thus he had no reason to look further back in the memory card.

Honey felt impatience at the waiting and uncertainty, but she wondered why she should care. It was not as if she liked Kate a lot. It would be no skin off her nose if Phil came across the proof of his wife's infidelity. But Kate had offered her friendship unasked and comfort when comfort was needed. She was a friend of sorts and when an almost-friend sought her help it would have been against both her fellow feeling and her professional pride not to do her utmost. Besides, Honey thought wryly, we all need somebody to look down on.

On the Thursday morning, she returned from a visit to her doctor to the news that Jock Briar wanted her to call him back. Her mind was full of other news. Her milk being almost over, she had been given an injection to halt the remaining trickle. Minka would have to make do with the offerings of other mammals while her mother, who had been patient for long enough, would at last have freedom to get out and about, unencumbered.

Once she had conveyed the news to June, who was delighted to realize that she would now be the major player in Minka's care and maintenance, she decided to return Mr Briar's call.

Jock Briar answered the phone in person. 'Mrs Laird,' he said. 'I have done my best. I have put the word about that your friend is offering a reward for the return of the memory card and that you'll put the boot in if anyone tries to be clever. There's only one man – well, a couple really, man and woman – who are regularly in the market for photies that might have value for the black, or as porn. I'm assuming that that's what we're talking about?' He waited, but Honey made no comment. 'Right. They've heard nothing and they promised me they'll let me have first offer if it turns up. I suppose they can't recognize it without looking at what's in it?'

'Knowing the man it belongs to, I'm sure that his postcode will be on it – the same postcode as mine. Now come to the point, Jock. Pee or get off the pot. Is this just to report no progress?'

'No' quite,' Jock said. 'It's to say that my assistant tells me the camera was bought by

Jem Tanar. The card was still in it. He paid cash.'

Honey glanced out of the window but no pigs were to be seen in flight. Jem Tanar was a shoplifter, teenage or very little more, who specialized in minor items of jewellery. Honey had come across him in the process of another and more pressing investigation and had not been impressed. That the young tearaway would part with cash for a camera was improbable; more likely was that in the process of haggling over the disposal of some booty he had ended up accepting the camera as part payment. That Jock Briar was prepared to name names suggested that Jock was worried.

'You've been in touch with him?' she asked.

'No' really. I've left messages for him, warning him to get in touch, but devil a word have I had back. His ma hasn't seen him. I've put the word around his cronies. I can't do more. I thought it best to warn you.'

Looking at it from Jock's point of view, Honey could see a degree of logic. It was certainly better to warn her than to let things slide. 'All right, Jock,' she said. 'I'll take it from here.'

Once again she had recourse to her premier investigative tool, the telephone. She put the word around her colleagues that she

33

wanted to see Jem Tanar. He seemed at first to have dropped out of sight, but after a day or two a CID sergeant tipped her off that young Tanar, for activities that even his broadminded mother would not have approved, rented a room in a tenement flat behind Ferry Road.

Honey knew that Sergeant Blair had a magic but strictly illegal touch with locks. 'Would you meet me there?' she asked.

'Delighted.' The sergeant had a special soft spot for Honey. 'What time?'

Pippa would be in need of a walk. 'Give me an hour.'

'It's a date,' Sergeant Blair said wistfully. Clearly he wished that it were so.

Honey's first call was in the kitchen. 'I have to go out,' she told June. 'Keep pouring milk into the Mighty Midget until told to stop. I'm taking Pippa.'

The day was grey and the wind was cold, but Pippa was delighted to be walked around the observatory again, an area that had been deemed to be too steep for Honey during the latter stages of her pregnancy. Honey was glad to stretch her legs again and to admire the view across the Firth of Forth to the Kingdom of Fife. The Range Rover still arrived at the given address precisely on time. Sergeant Blair's unmarked Corsa dead-heated with her.

The tenement rose grim-faced from the usual bald and impersonal Edinburgh street, a canyon through solid buildings, made narrower by the vehicles parked and apparently abandoned on each side. The stairway was well above average, being swept, recently painted and smelling of almost nothing but disinfectant. Honey took Pippa with her for little reason other than that Pippa had an ultra-sensitive nose for scents that might be of interest to the police. Additionally, it gave Honey confidence to be accompanied by a large, black dog although Pippa had a soft mouth and a gentle heart. Two floors up they came to a dark blue door embellished by a simple number. With the sergeant on one side of her and Pippa on the other, Honey knocked. There was no reply and no neighbour showed any interest. The silence was oppressive. She knocked more loudly.

The sergeant leaned against the door and did something out of Honey's sight. 'I do believe they've gone out and left the place unlocked,' he said. 'Very careless. I think I'll step inside and leave them a note to warn them to be more careful.'

'I think you should do just that,' Honey said.

The lobby of the flat was small and stuffy.

The flat itself was very small. It had been decorated cheaply and by an amateur hand but by somebody with a good eye for colour. An open door showed a sitting room furnished with four unmatched fireside chairs and nothing else. There was a simple kitchen equipped, apart from the usual fittings and a minimum of white goods, with a kettle and a pathetic array of breakfast dishes and materials for one person. There was neither the smell nor the residual warmth of cooking.

Another open door led to a bedroom holding a tidily made bed, a lightweight chair and a wardrobe. Pippa was pulling hard, her claws scraping on the bare linoleum. Honey wanted to look inside the other bedroom but she caught the sergeant's eye and nodded at the closed door. Then she let Pippa pull her into the first bedroom. The Labrador had suffered only elementary and basic training but had learned by human praise and rewards what was to be expected – at a crime scene as well as in the shooting field – and her sudden determination was not to be ignored.

Pippa took a seat in front of the locked wardrobe and would not be budged. Honey called back the officer.

DS Blair arrived back in the doorway. 'You'd better take a look in there, Inspector,' he said indicating the other room.

'I will. That's what I came for. I'll look in there if you look in here. Pippa doesn't usually make mistakes.'

Blair seemed to be on the point of objecting but he shrugged suddenly. The door to the other bedroom was standing ajar. She stopped in the opening. One glance was enough. She had only set eyes on Jem Tanar once before, but she had not forgotten the blunt head with outthrust jaw and crooked teeth nor the slicked-down hair. It was undoubtedly his body, very much deceased, that lay on the single, unmade bed. It wore jeans and a white T-shirt. The T-shirt now exhibited the slits and stains from three stab wounds, any one of which, it seemed to Honey, would have been fatal. The blood was black and mostly dry. It had puddled on the bedclothes. Even if he had been stabbed elsewhere, which was unlikely, he had certainly died where he lay.

It rushed through Honey's mind that the outlook was not good. It was bad for Kate's hopes of keeping her secret safe. It was bad for Honey's prospect of preserving her maternity leave intact. The outlook for the owner of the flat was worst of all – except, of course for Jem Tanar, for whom the doom had already arrived.

Four

Honey had seen many bodies in the course of her duties. At first, she had been horrified, empathizing bitterly with the deceased. In time she had learned to treat the body as just one more clue – a piece of meat that could tell a story. Usually, in the normal course of a detective's job, she had been called after death had occurred and been certified; and however gruesome the scene she knew that it was there and could brace herself for it. The shock of the unpleasant and unexpected scene first took her breath away and then caused a sudden nausea. This had not yet been confirmed as a dead body. Part of her mind was sure of it and yet she suffered a primitive fear that if it moved ... Anger followed – not at the death but at the sudden break in the chain of her enquiries. She pulled herself together and returned to the other bedroom.

She was confronted by a scene that nearly pushed murder into second place. Pippa was still sitting where Honey had left her. DS

Blair had opened the wall cupboard. It contained a stack of several white packets, some other materials, a chemical balance and a few of what seemed to be mixing tools. It took little effort to guess that this was the headquarters of a major drug distributor. Apart from the open door and the presence of two people and a dog, the room was totally tidy and the air smelled fresh as though the occupant had been absent for a few days.

'The chiefs won't be too happy with the corp next door,' DS Blair said, 'but they'll be delighted with this lot.'

'I expect so. Have you phoned in?'

The sergeant seemed surprised. 'Me? It's your case and you're the senior officer. I only came along...'

'To unlock doors? Are you going to tell them that? Never mind. Do you have a radio?'

DS Blair surrendered his radio. Honey called in to report the body. 'We need the police surgeon, a pathologist, somebody from the Drug Squad, SOCO and whichever senior officer is going to take on the case. The procurator fiscal should be told. I'm here on a completely different matter and I'm still on maternity leave. I brought DS Blair along to keep it official.' Detective Sergeant Blair raised an approving thumb. 'I'll remain here for the moment as a witness.'

After a short delay, she was told that the police surgeon was on his way.

'I strongly recommend,' Honey said, 'that no marked vehicles are shown in the vicinity and no personnel in uniform. The principal occupier of the flat may not know about the body. The body is already dead whereas a live drug dealer is still walking around. We should spread the net for him.'

'I'll pass it on,' said the voice.

Honey took Pippa down to the Range Rover. She phoned June to say that she was caught up in a fresh case and would come home when she could. June sounded pleased. They were interrupted by a fresh radio message. Detective Chief Inspector Gilchrist would be taking charge. Detective Inspector Laird was to remain in charge pending his arrival, maternity leave notwithstanding.

There came a rap on the window. One of the local doctors, frequently called on to act as a police surgeon, had recognized her or the car. She got out. 'Doctor Wiseman,' she said.

'Detective Inspector Honeypot.'

Honey pretended to give him a knee in the groin but cut the move short. The doctor grinned. He was a clean and tidy man in his thirties, well spoken and well mannered. He had a habit of needling Honey but in a friendly and almost affectionate manner, so

40

she refused to allow his use of her despised nickname to rile her. She led him up to the flat, carefully closing the entry door behind them. She placed DS Blair on a chair behind the door with orders to check the identity of every arrival and to detain anyone without identification as being of the police.

The doctor studied the body, checked the temperature and examined the eyes and the wounds.

'He's dead,' he pronounced first. 'You could see that for yourselves but it has to be certified. He's been dead a couple of days, give or take quite a lot. The stab wounds are obvious and could have been fatal. I can't see any other possible cause of death without disturbing the body in a manner that would send your pathologist nuts. No smell of drink or signs of drugs. No marks of ligatures or bruising. That's all, folks.' He left a smile to be shared between Honey, Sergeant Blair and the corpse and went about his business.

The next arrival was a sergeant in the Drug Squad. He had recently arrived in Edinburgh, transferred from Strathclyde, and was unknown to either Honey or Sergeant Blair. The two sergeants nearly came to blows until identities were established; but thereafter the newcomer's delight in the treasure trove was such that the men were soon buddies. The newcomer reported to his own department – Honey gathered that there was joy in heaven – and took over duty at the flat door.

The trickle of arrivals became almost a flood. The pathologist and a photographer sidled around each other until the state of the body was fully recorded. The removal of the body was organized so discreetly that the mortuary vehicle was only at the door for a matter of seconds. DCI Gilchrist had arrived by then and made his own inspection of the body. He unleashed his team of SOCOs to make a total search and record of the flat. Anyone in white overalls was, he said, to remain clear of the uncurtained windows or keep below sill level.

He took Honey into the sitting room, which seemed to have seen little use except perhaps as a venue for business deals. They sat on opposite sides of a dummy fireplace like a long established couple. The flat was cold so Honey switched on the electric fire and mentally damned any change to the status quo that might occur.

The chief inspector was near retirement. Honey guessed that this level of seniority entitled him to conduct a murder investigation but that if the case escalated in complexity or in publicity value he would find a superintendent put in over his head. Honey had noticed that few people retain the figure of their earlier years but either run to bulk or become lean and stringy. DCI Gilchrist was following the latter course and his face was almost unlined so that he looked much younger than his real years. This was sometimes an advantage and sometimes the opposite. Beneath his silver thatch Gilchrist's smooth face was both rosy and tanned, giving him the same appearance of reversed tones as an African with bleached hair. His manner remained fatherly. Honey had been warned that he was a stickler and that his temper was uncertain, but she thought that she might prefer him to her usual *bête noir*, Detective Superintendent Blackhouse.

'Explain to me, please,' he said, 'how you come to be here.'

Honey had had time to choose her words. 'Although, as you know, I'm on maternity leave,' she said, 'I was approached by a friend of mine with a problem. Her house had been burgled and her husband's camera stolen. She was not too worried about the camera itself, but it held photographs of an unrepeatable occasion. It is a digital camera and she wanted the memory card back. I put the word around that there would be a reward for the return of the camera and it was indeed returned, but without the memory card. An informant, under promise of confidentiality, told me that the camera, complete with card, had at some time been in the hands of Jem Tanar, the boy through there. I came here to find out about it and I brought Sergeant Blair with me to be the official presence should any *situation* arise. I should point out that I'm here as a witness and not as an officer, but I would be eternally grateful if—'

She was interrupted. A large man in jeans and a hairy sweater carrying a haversack had unsuspectingly entered the lobby of the flat. Seeing all the activity, he had turned to flee, but had been pounced on. It took the combined efforts of Sergeant Blair, the sergeant from the Drug Squad and one of the SOCOs to bring him under control, by which time his haversack had spilled more white packets and some white powder. He was handcuffed and born off in triumph. A forensic technician was set to clearing up the scattered powder.

Honey and the chief inspector resumed their seats. 'You were promising eternal gratitude,' he reminded her.

'It seems,' Honey said, 'that I have already earned undying gratitude by uncovering the den of a major drug dealer. I was promising to invest some of that gratitude in you if you would get the searchers to look particularly for a Viking Interworks SD memory card.

It's very small. About an inch by an inch and a quarter and it would have a postcode written on the back, probably in ultraviolet security pen.'

He regarded her dispassionately for a few seconds. 'They should spot it,' he said at last. 'If I read you right, you seem to be asking for special treatment because you chanced on evidence of a drug dealer. I suppose we owe you something for your sensible suggestion that we set a trap. Now you'd better go and leave me to interview the last arrival. To save police time, write out a statement of all you know. You must be well aware of the form.'

'I'd prefer to be present during the search, just as an observer.'

'In this case, and at this point in it,' said the chief inspector, 'you are a witness and nothing more.' She thought that he had nearly added *my girl*. 'Who was your informant?' he asked casually.

'I'm not at liberty to say.'

He nodded. It was understood that the identities of informants could be kept absolutely confidential. The flow of information would be cut off if informants were at risk of their identities becoming known.

The flow of information within police headquarters was still rapid and all embracing. Honey had barely returned home before

45

Detective Superintendent Blackhouse was on the phone. 'What's this I hear about you getting involved in somebody else's case?'

'I decided to spend a few hours of my maternity leave –' she put emphasis on the two words – 'trying to help a friend to recover some stolen goods. I found the body of the man I wanted to speak to. He had been stabbed. I'm a witness but not involved in the enquiries. As the finder of the body, I'm probably a suspect.'

This flippancy was rightly ignored. 'You seem to be involving yourself in some other enquiries. It seems you're quite fit to return to duty. You already took some maternity leave before the birth.'

Honey had picked up the call in the cluttered study and was perched uncomfortably in the hard swivel chair. She had already learned that if she knuckled down to the superintendent he would walk all over her. On the other hand, if she stood up to him he would crumble – she really must take more care with her metaphors, she told herself. Sandy was inclined to laugh at her when she scrambled them so utterly. 'And during that period,' she retorted, 'you asked me to undertake some enquiries for you on the understanding that that time would not count against my maternity leave. I brought those enquiries to a successful conclusion

46

and have spent some of the succeeding time in writing statements and precognitions and directing the processes of case preparation. A tribunal might decide that my maternity leave hadn't even started yet. You'll have to excuse me now, your goddaughter is crying for her mother. Sir,' she added as an afterthought.

The silence at the other end of the line was broken only by a faint sound as of a detective superintendent taking deep breaths. She thought that he might also be grinding his teeth. She disconnected. She settled herself more comfortably before phoning Kate Ingliston to break the bad news. 'But cheer up,' she told Kate. 'The searchers may find it.'

'Oh God! I hope so,' Kate said. There was, Honey noted, no mention of shock or horror at the grisly death. 'If they do, can you get it back for me without any of them looking at it?'

'I have requested exactly that. Which may be all that was needed to make sure that one of them has a peep. But I don't suppose that any of them know you by sight.'

'Oh God, Honey, please be joking.' Silence on the line was only broken by a loud sniff. 'Do you think he was killed by somebody who wanted to get hold of my memory card? Have you let him make off with it?'

That idea had never occurred to Honey.

On the face of it, it was ridiculous. But Kate was overdue for a little more needling, Honey decided, for involving her in all this fuss and flap by being so indiscreet about her amours – and indeed for having the amours in the first place. And enjoying them: that was the ultimate sin. 'It's possible,' she said. 'Luckily I can account for my time over the last few days. I hope that you and your boyfriend can do the same. You do make the obvious suspects. If he gets called...'

'Now you're pulling my leg,' Kate said. 'He couldn't have anything to do with it.'

'But a defence lawyer might well use him as a red herring.'

'How would a defence lawyer know anything about him?'

'It is an obligation on the prosecution to reveal to the defence any facts that might contribute to the defence case.' Honey disconnected. 'And how does that grab you?' she asked the dead phone.

Five

According to DCI Gilchrist, when they spoke next day, the searchers were adamant that they had gone through the flat with a thoroughness that would have disclosed individual fleas, and without finding anything of more interest than the drugs and evidence of some very strange sexual habits on the part of Jem Tanar. There was certainly no sign of a memory card. Honey had no reason to disbelieve either Gilchrist or the searchers. The card had little intrinsic value and she had stuck to the story that its value to the proper owner arose only from sentiment.

Honey believed Kate to be praying, perhaps offering to change her ways if only her maker would save her from disaster. Honey felt a certain curiosity as to the exact wording of the prayer but could not find an excuse for asking. Kate seemed to be in fear of public humiliation more than her husband's wrath and kept her fingers crossed. Honey was awaiting a suitable opportunity to mention that if Kate had kept everything crossed instead of just her fingers her present anxiety need not have arisen. There are certain advantages in having a friend whose friendship is not particularly valued; freedom to speak out is the foremost of them.

Honey rather felt that she had put out enough effort on behalf of her undeserving neighbour. She did retain enough interest to phone DCI Gilchrist to suggest that the drug peddler and official tenant of the flat might well know how young Tanar had come by the camera and how he had disposed of it. But the word that came back was that that individual would only say that he hadn't the faintest idea and that if he did know he would rather be drowned in something unrepeatable than say a single word to the filthy fuzz who were trying to frame him for possession of substances that he did not possess, with intent to supply, which he never intended in the first place. And who was going to reimburse him for the value of the confiscated stock? They could not link him with what had happened to his flatmate, he said, because he had been away for the past week visiting his auntie in ... in Bognor.

Honey clung to her belief that Tanar had acquired the camera as part of a dodgy deal and that his killer had made off with it.

After that, she tried to put the matter out

of her mind. She had quite enough to think about. One of Sandy's long-running cases, concerning suspected corruption in connection with a proposed oil refinery, was beginning to gather momentum and he was trying to be in three places at once. The Lairds had planned to take a Mediterranean break during Honey's maternity leave but Sandy felt duty bound to see the case through until charges were filed. Honey was wondering how to juggle her own leisure when fate played into her hands. One of her colleagues broke both legs in a skiing accident and Detective Superintendent Blackhouse found himself without a trustworthy assistant to take charge of a minor but difficult case of arson and fraud. Honey allowed herself to be persuaded to do a turn of duty in exchange for the superintendent's promise – a written promise, this time around – of time off in lieu.

On the morning of her third day back at work, she was leaving the house when she met the postwoman almost on the doorstep. Honey would have shot past, uttering a quick 'Good morning, postie', but the lady stopped her, putting out an earnest hand well speckled with liver spots and reminding Honey of the Ancient Mariner. 'Mrs Laird,' she said, 'somebody posted this in a box in Haddington. It has your postcode on it. As a police officer, I thought you'd maybe be the right person to take charge of it.' She produced a memory card for a digital camera. The postcode was written on it neatly, in white ink.

Honey was en route to a meeting with the fire officers and the forensic science team. These were in profound disagreement with each other. Honey hated above all things to be late for any engagement and she was preoccupied with what she would have to say in the hope of bringing the discordant factions together. She acknowledged the small device with a word or two, wrapped it in a paper tissue and dropped it into the suede shoulder bag that she invariably carried during the daytime. She refused to begin rejoicing. Digital memories can be copied and Kate's image, in full colour and action, might already be circulating in some adult magazine. She put it out of her mind and concentrated on her arguments for the meeting to come, which turned out to be at least as fraught as Honey had feared. She managed to tiptoe between rival arguments and in the end sent both sides on their ways, each believing themselves to have gained the upper hand.

The memory card might have remained indefinitely in Honey's bag, forgotten among the handcuff and other keys, mobile phone, pager, notebooks, ball-point pens, old lipstick cases and suchlike trivia that tend to accumulate in the bags of even the most meticulous of female police inspectors. But the keys of the Range Rover had somehow escaped from the internal side-pocket, necessitating a more thorough search. Her eye passed over the tissue but a tiny mental bell began to tinkle and that evening, after paying her usual call on her daughter, she repeated the search and unwrapped the memory card, handling it carefully with gloved hands.

At that moment, temptation raised its head. During her youth, Honey had been sure that temptation only existed for the pleasure of yielding to it. What else, she asked herself, was it *for*? Since her escalation in the ranks of the police and also her marriage to Sandy, she had modified her view and now believed that the pleasure entailed was the glow of virtue in resisting it. She had surprised herself by becoming quite resolute in her resistance to its lures, but after all it was neither greed nor lust that was tempting her now, but mere curiosity. Considering the question over her first G and T of the evening, she decided that curiosity was an essentially feminine weakness and that she was therefore entitled, almost obliged, to indulge it.

She booted up the computer, inserted the card into the card-reader and waited for the images to load. The computer's monitor screen began to show enlarged, sharp images. A few seconds sufficed to flick past Phil Ingliston's photographs and to arrive at the subject of Kate's concern. There could be no doubt that Kate and her paramour, whose face seemed vaguely familiar, had indulged themselves, running the gamut of sexual experience. Honey had just decided that this was too good to keep to herself when she heard Sandy's key in the front door. Honey intercepted him in the hall and while he disposed of his coat, hat and outdoor shoes she gave him a brief résumé of her morning. The discovery of a body by a working detective, while not commonplace, is not unknown and Sandy, while Honey steered his slippered feet in the direction of the study, refused to get excited.

'I have Kate's memory card here,' Honey said. 'I was just wondering whether to have a quick look at it. Just to be sure that it really is hers, you understand. June says that dinner will be half an hour yet.'

Sandy thought it over, showing rather more interest than he had in the fatal stabbing. Honey had kept him abreast of the story as it unfolded. 'The proper course would be to offer it to Kate and let her tell

54

you whether the images are hers,' he said. He paused and his face took on that first pale hint of a grin that she knew to be his look of imminent mischief. 'But that would entail allowing a member of the public to view images that may not be hers, or even her husband's. We never cared a lot about proper courses. I'll get a chair and a dram. Then let's have a look and see what all the fuss was about.'

'I hoped you'd say that.'

'I knew you did.'

Together they scrolled through the slide show. Phil had cleared most of the memory when he'd last printed the images and transferred them to floppy disc. The first few new images were his professional records of inspected work. Then they arrived at the meat. Considering the limitations of the light and the lens, the camera had done a remarkable job. Honey had already seen the images once but Sandy was stunned. 'It's the Kama Sutra in black suspenders,' he said. 'I'm seeing Kate Ingliston in an entirely new light.'

'And seeing more of her than you've ever seen before, I hope, and from some rather unusual angles. Sandy, she must never know that we've peeped.'

'No, of course not.'

The close of the bedroom series had been signalled by a shot of the frontage of a build-

ing. Sandy said, 'Scroll on further. Somebody must have used the camera while it was
in wrong hands. It could be relevant to your
other case.'

'By a considerable stretch of the imagination, I suppose it could.' Honey scrolled
forward. A few shots of buildings and
scenery showed. The people seemed to be
accidental inclusions until one figure kept
turning up. It was that of a black girl in a
white dress, showing very white teeth as she
smiled at the camera.

Honey's finger moved again. The image on
the monitor changed. A black girl, presumably the same one, lay face down on a
bright bedcover in front of a window. She
was naked and the handle of a knife stood up
from her back. She had been stabbed once.

Honey scrolled on. There were more images but only of people and buildings and
nothing more to get a conscientious police
officer excited.

'I never said that we should ignore it,' Honey
protested. She lowered her voice. They were
in the middle of dinner but what they were
discussing was not for the ears of June.
'What I was trying to say, between inter-
ruptions, was that we now know of two fatal
stabbings, which suggests either a connection or a remarkable coincidence. But

pictures of our neighbour frolicking bare-arsed with an unknown fancy man can hardly be relevant to either case. If we let those pictures get into the public domain I give it two hours before they're on the Internet.'

Sandy put down his knife and fork, carefully aligned. 'Even if that were true, and I can't deny that it's a possibility, that doesn't entitle us to withhold evidence.'

Honey had to clench her teeth to prevent her voice rising. 'I have still not suggested that we withhold evidence. I am trying to point out to whoever will listen – a category of person that seems to be lacking here and now – that those specific photographs aren't evidence of anything except the enterprise, ingenuity and immorality of our friend and her partner. It does seem a pity to shatter a marriage for so negative a reason.'

'On the contrary,' said Sandy, 'those photographs are the best possible evidence that that marriage isn't worth a damn. Were you prepared to chance your career for the sake of the obviously shaky marriage of somebody neither of us likes very much? What would you suggest?'

'I was hoping to receive constructive suggestions from yourself, but that seems to be increasingly unlikely. My immediate thought was to erase that series of images and let our colleagues have the rest.'

They were interrupted by June bringing in and serving the sweet course. When they had the room to themselves again Sandy said, 'I couldn't go along with that. Sod's Law being what it is, the gentleman in those photographs would turn out to be the brother of the male corpse and the boyfriend of the female one. I could accept transferring everything except the sex shots to a disc or another card and letting them have that. You would then have to store away the original card, admitting that it exists but declining to produce it unless evidence turns up to connect anything in those photographs to either case.'

'I could do that,' Honey said.

'I admit that you have a stubborn streak as wide as the Firth of Forth but I don't think you appreciate the kind of pressure you'd be under. I have a better idea. Copy the whole card but obliterate the two faces.'

'There you are,' Honey said triumphantly. 'I told you that you'd come up with something constructive if I asked you often enough.'

'No, you didn't.'

'Well, I was going to. Come into the study and you can give me a hand.'

'Must I? You're perfectly competent.'

'Thank you. But I'm not very experienced.

I couldn't be sure of blurring the faces without doing more damage than that.'

Sandy showed signs of embarrassment. 'I don't know that I could sit in front of those images for long without getting overexcited.'

Honey looked at him sharply but he seemed to be serious. 'So much the better,' she said. 'You don't get overexcited as often as I could wish. Come on.'

Six

Honey's return to Fettes Avenue HQ and duty was not a plunge into the excitement of a baffling investigation, but into dull routine. From the first, there had been no room to doubt that the proprietor of the premises had been responsible for the fraud and arson. He had not even contrived a credible explanation for an accidental fire and he had increased his insurance only a month earlier. Honey's small team, comprising for the moment one sergeant, a constable, a civilian collator and occasionally a lady from the procurator fiscal's office, was concerned with ferreting out the details of the operation and assembling legal proof. The next steps in this process were already obvious. Her part in the case was about as interesting, Honey told her husband, as being helmsman on a railway train.

She escaped early from her morning's progress meeting. DCI Gilchrist was still in his own meeting, struggling to ensure that every member of his team knew what every other member had uncovered and what to do next. A cautious phone call had revealed that Gilchrist was responsible, in this case, to Detective Superintendent Blackhouse. Honey decided to start with her bête noire.

Mr Blackhouse was in the habit of keeping a short queue waiting for audience with him. He felt that it added to his dignity. For a similar reason, the room had been rather better decorated and equipped, at his own expense, than the average office for his rank. It was ten minutes or so before Honey was admitted to the sanctum. As usual, she was greeted as though she had been his personal invention although she was quite prepared for, and might even have welcomed, a sudden fall out of favour. But no. An invitation to be seated showed that she was still flavour of the month. Others, less favoured, would be left to stand. She first made a brief report on the fraud and arson case and the superintendent was pleased to approve the swift progress made towards a conclusion.

Then Honey got down to her real business. 'As you know,' she said, 'I was approached by a neighbour in connection with a missing camera. Following up information, I found the body of Jem Tanar. That's now DCI Gilchrist's case. The camera was recovered but the memory card had vanished. The memory card has now reached my hands. It

61

had been dropped into a postbox in Haddington.' She was about to explain the coincidence of postcodes but realized just in time that, given such information, any curious officer could easily home in on Kate Ingliston. 'The postie brought it to me. In search of evidence, I examined it.'

She produced an envelope and took out a wad of 10 x 15cm paper. 'The first four shots are the work of my friend's husband, recording work that he was supervising.' She passed them over. The superintendent leafed through them quickly and pushed them aside. 'The next nineteen,' Honey said, 'are the reason why my friend was so anxious to recover the camera.'

The detective superintendent took some time leafing through the second set, his eyebrows rising ever higher towards his bald pate. It was several minutes before he suddenly asked, 'What happened to the faces?'

'I purposely blurred all the features. I felt that I had to bring you the photographs because of what follows but I am not prepared to reveal the identity of my friend unless and until it is shown to be relevant. You see, while the camera was out of our hands, somebody took another twelve photographs. You should look at them.'

Mr Blackhouse looked quickly through the set of photographs showing the black girl until he came to the last of those images. He uttered a strangled snort. 'Good God! Is this genuine?'

'I've looked at it in full magnification. If it's a fake it's a very clever one.'

'Why come to me instead of to DCI Gilchrist? It seems to tie in with his case.'

'DCI Gilchrist,' Honey said, 'would undoubtedly insist on knowing the identity of my neighbour, which I am not prepared to reveal. I hoped that you might support me in allowing an otherwise respectable member of the citizenry, whose husband has a certain position to keep up, to remain anonymous. I don't mind giving the rest of the world a cheap thrill but the least I can do for a friend is to hide her identity unless it turns out to be relevant – which at the moment seems inconceivable.'

The detective superintendent seemed amused. He could thunder with genuine indignation when citizens stepped outside what the law allowed but he was inclined to betray cynical or even salacious amusement when the sexual frailties of the respectable were brought to his attention. 'I'll back you that far,' he said. 'I only hope you'd do as much for me.'

'Of course I would,' Honey said, her fingers crossed under the desk. 'But I can hardly believe that it will ever be necessary.'

Mr Blackhouse hesitated. Honey thought that he might be considering whether to accept her comment as praise for his morals or resent it as a slight on his sexual appeal. 'What did you make of the scenery?' he asked

Honey had spent some time in studying the background. Recognizing a scene can be difficult until the viewer is oriented, but those few shots in which the sun was shining gave her the first clue. As soon as she was sure that the main focus of the photographs was looking south across a large stretch of water, the answer became obvious. 'Moray and Beauly Firths, looking south,' Honey said promptly. 'You can recognize Inverness and the new suspension bridge in the distance. I know the area well.'

Mr Blackhouse closed his eyes for most of a minute. The uninformed observer might have thought him asleep, but Honey knew that he was thinking hard. She also knew that, while he was not a great detective, he was an able administrator. He was a rare example of a man promoted into, rather than out of, what he did well. Whatever he came up with would make sense. 'Who's assisting you on the arson?' he asked suddenly.

'Detective Sergeant Jessop.'

'And the procurator fiscal?'

'Mrs Bland.'

'Do they work well together?'

'They make a good team.' Honey had sometimes thought that if the two made any better a team she would have to throw a bucket of water over them.

'Then leave them in charge of putting together the case for the prosecution. You're the only officer available who knows the territory and you've liaised with the Northern Constabulary before now. You take on the case of this black girl and do the liaison with Northern. Work with DCI Gilchrist on the other killing, but our end of this one is your case. You'll have to walk very carefully if you're not going to tread on the corns of either Northern or DCI Gilchrist. And – Inspector – the last time you stayed overnight in the Inverness area...' Mr Blackhouse broke off. He seemed unsure how to proceed. His bulk was fidgeting uncomfortably.

'Sir?' Honey could guess what was coming. A whisper had reached her from a friend in the audit office.

'You slept in what must be the most expensive hotel in Europe. You won't get away with that again. I had to fight tooth and nail to save your skin last time.'

Honey brought her mind back from contemplation of the lovely night she'd spent in that hotel. 'I didn't know that,' she said. 'I'm grateful. But I paid for the upgrade myself.'

'Oh.' Clearly the superintendent had not been told. Somebody in Finance had been using her journey as an excuse to make his life difficult. Now he was smiling. The Somebody in Finance, she thought, was going to get his head in his hands. 'Did you indeed? Go and spell it out for the arson team,' he said. 'Come back in about an hour.'

Detective Sergeant Jessop and Mrs Bland were still in earnest discussion. The sergeant was placidly accepting her instructions. They were surprised but neither seemed unhappy about the altered responsibilities.

Honey returned to the superintendant's room at the conclusion of the allotted hour. Mr Blackhouse seemed more animated than usual. 'There was a black girl reported missing from the hostel run by the Young Women's Presbyterian Association,' he announced.

'I'll check,' Honey answered.

The switchboard connected her to a number for the police headquarters in Inverness. But no, there had been no reports of a young black woman being stabbed, to death or otherwise, not in recent years or indeed anywhere north of Grampian where, the voice seemed to suggest, anything could be expected to happen. Honey thanked her informant and obtained both a fax number and the email address before disconnecting.

'So now,' said the detective superintendent gloomily, 'I suppose you'll be making a case for a trip north.'

Honey glanced out of the window. The winter had been mild but a few flakes of snow were now promising a change. She sighed. Sorrento would be beautiful just now. Perhaps a little later when Sandy was free of his present caseload. 'First things first,' she said. 'I'd better ask the YWPA warden, or whatever they call them, to identify the girl from the photograph. Then I'll send Northern a report and a copy of the photographs. Let them do the running around.'

Mr Blackhouse nodded. 'I like your way of thinking,' he said.

Seven

Just in case the relevance of the photographs should ever become proven or somebody around chief constable level was to intervene, Honey had brought the memory card, carefully wrapped, in her shoulder bag. It took her only a matter of minutes to abstract the photographs of the mysterious girl and to incorporate them into an email. Drafting a report and request for assistance took rather longer. She had intended to do no more than to explain that the attached photographs had been found on a stolen and recovered digital camera. But it had been necessary to add an explanation of the young woman missing from the YWPA hostel, in order to ensure that Edinburgh was kept advised of whatever was learned. She decided not to make mention of Jem Tanar yet.

She left the electronic image of her completed email on the typing pool computer, for despatch on her command, and went out. The snow had begun but there was not yet the rise in temperature often associated with the beginning of snowfall and, with a gusty breeze whipping around the buildings, the feeling was of bitter cold. The YWPA hostel was in a street where a previous Range Rover had been vandalized and, moreover, it would be at serious risk of being skidded into by the less experienced drivers of Edinburgh. She had bespoken transport by panda car. She was chauffeured to the door of the hostel by a cheerful woman constable.

The YWPA hostel had been built with some other purpose in mind, perhaps in connection with business or education. A panel over the entrance door looked as though it had originally held a proud statement of the function of the building but had later been chiselled smooth. The frontage was of local stone but elaborately fashioned with carvings that were Grecian in style. As the car pulled up, she saw that the main door was protected by a good security lock and an entryphone system. She hated taking advantage of her seniority but rank has its privileges. She asked the driver, very nicely and politely, to go and obtain admission for her. The driver, now rather less cheerful than before, said something under her breath that Honey pretended not to hear but she got out of the car and slithered over the icy paving to the door. As Honey had suspected, it took some minutes before anyone spoke from inside on the entryphone and longer still for the driver to establish that a very important police person wanted ingress and would be very angry if her driver were kept standing in the falling snow for much longer.

The latch must have clicked at last, because Honey saw the driver push the door open and hold it with her foot. The driver, when Honey reached the door, was looking even less cheerful. 'Thank you,' Honey said. 'Now, go and get dried and warmed up.' The driver was not used to superiors who thanked her or gave a damn whether she was warm and dry or deep-frozen. She smiled shyly and hurried back into the car.

The door had been opened by a woman in an overall who looked Honey up and down. She had a mean face and a drip on her nose and she obviously intended to be as obstructive as she could manage without laying herself open to a riposte. 'You don't look like a policewoman,' she said. She made no attempt to move aside and let Honey in.

Honey was not amused. She put her identification almost up against the other's nose, at the same time leaning and stepping forward so that the other was forced to retreat.

'Satisfied?'

'I suppose so,' the woman said reluctantly.

'I want to see the boss-lady. What is she

called? The warden?'

'This isn't Miss Morrison's time for seeing people.' She closed the door but her manner managed to suggest that this was to keep the snow out rather than to accept that Honey was now inside and intended to stay there. She remained between Honey and the hall-way.

Honey had had years of experience with self-important and obstructive people. 'But it is *my* time for seeing people,' she said. 'Miss Morrison is first on my list; and the requirements of the police take priority. Go and tell her so.' The woman hesitated. Honey was tempted to take out of her bag, first a notebook, then a pen and finally a pair of handcuffs. It had worked in the past but she thought that this woman might well call her bluff. 'Get on with it,' she said.

The woman turned away, sniffing. Bypass-ing the broad staircase, she set off along a dark passage, her back registering anger and contempt. She turned a corner and left Honey to contemplate the gloomy hall. This had been hung with several pictures of an obliquely religious nature and was domin-ated by a large, dark painting of several fully clad ladies reclining on cushions around a low table laden with fruit. There was no label to suggest what historical or possibly biblical scene this was intended to represent. The building was old, with high ceilings, Greek key pattern around the cornice and a great deal of dark pitch pine. The floor was of black and white tiles, like a public lavatory. Soon the sound of footsteps returned and Honey was joined by a chubby lady just entering middle age. She had a vague smile overlying a look of surprise. 'Detective Inspector Laird?'

'That's so. Miss Morrison?'

'Yes. Can I help you? What is it about?'

Honey produced a print of one of the better photographs of the black girl, alive. 'Do you recognize this young lady?'

The smile disappeared altogether, like that of the Cheshire cat. Miss Morrison took the whole sheaf of photographs and leafed through it. Honey retained only the shot that included the knife. The woman who had admitted Honey was trying hard to look over Miss Morrison's shoulder but Honey and the warden combined to give her a quelling look and she retreated.

'I'm just checking to see if she has a sort of birthmark beside her eye,' Miss Morrison said. 'The photographer seems to have tried to keep it out of the picture, but she does. That's Harriet Benskin. She had no papers with her, but she had clearly been brought up Church of Scotland so I could hardly turn her away. Has something happened to her? I know one of the girls reported her missing.'

'Possibly. So, you can confirm that she had a room here?'

'Half a room. She still has it, because her rent was paid up in advance. Would you like to see it or would you rather speak to me somewhere private?'

'Her room isn't private?'

'Her room-mate works as a temp and often works from here. I think she's in the room just now.'

'She may be able to help quite a lot. But first, please wait one moment.' Honey produced her mobile and keyed a single digit. She was connected to the typing pool and gave instructions that her email was to be sent. 'Now, shall we go?'

'There's some mail for her. Should I give it to you?'

'I'll collect it before I go.'

The room that Harriet Benskin had shared turned out to be both generous and airy, and brighter than the outside of the building would have suggested. The decor was fresh and contemporary. The furniture seemed small in the spacious room; but the bed and chairs looked comfortable, suggesting that they had been chosen for comfort rather than appearance.

The room-mate was a girl named Dorothy

Hall. Honey had been born without any tendency to put on weight. She was aware how lucky she had been and made a point of never deriding the overweight even in the privacy of her own mind, but there was no denying that Ms Hall was plump and well on the way towards being fat.

Miss Morrison perched on the bed. Dorothy retained the chair at the dressing table (which served also as a desk), leaving the wicker fireside chair to Honey. It creaked in a way that she found distracting.

'What's this about?' Dorothy asked. 'Is this to do with Harriet? *I* haven't done anything.' She was looking only mildly anxious. From the stacks of paper on the dressing table it was evident that she had done quite a lot, but nothing evidently meriting the attention of the police.

'Something's happened to Harriet,' said Miss Morrison. 'I don't know what yet. Detective Inspector Laird wanted to see the room and speak to you.'

Honey decided to use a minor euphemism rather than drop a bombshell. 'To cut a long story very, very short,' she said, 'it appears that Harriet may have suffered a fatal assault. We do not have a body although we can be fairly sure where it is. Anything you can tell us about her would be welcomed.'

Miss Morrison and Dorothy Hall exchanged a glance that combined horror with fascination. 'I saw very little of her,' said the warden. 'I interviewed her when she asked for a room, just to be sure that she was eligible – that means a member of a Presbyterian church – and that she wasn't going to be trouble. She seemed a nice, intelligent, well-read girl.'

'So she was,' said Dorothy. 'She was very neat and clean; not very cheerful, maybe a bit of a depressive. She had a mark on her face and a bit of a port wine stain beside her eye. She seemed a wee bit sensitive about it. Every other way, she was just like anybody. What else do you want to know? She was a good typist and I put some work her way. She was quite friendly but reserved, if you know what I mean, but not exactly a laugh a minute. I'm just the opposite, so I never got to know her well.'

'When did you last see her?'

'When I left for work, about a week ago. Wednesday morning, it must have been.'

Honey looked at Miss Morrison. The warden looked flustered. 'I think it was that day,' she said. 'Harriet left as though to go to a job but then came back at about lunchtime. There was a man with her. She said that she had only come back to collect some things. I wouldn't normally allow men upstairs; but in the middle of the day ... Anyway she didn't look as if there was anything ... amorous going on. About half an hour later she came skittering down the stairs and I saw her scribbling something at the hall table, on paper that she took from under her coat. Then the man came hurrying down after her. I didn't see the papers again—'

'That was the day all my papers were upside down,' Dorothy broke in. 'As if somebody'd been searching for something.'

'Quite probably,' Honey said. 'Was there anything among your papers that related to Miss Benskin? Or anything that could be of interest or value to anyone else?'

'I wish,' Dorothy said.

'Can you describe the man?' Honey asked the warden.

Miss Morrison looked uncertain. 'Not very well,' she said. 'He wasn't particularly tall but he was well built. Not fat, but burly. He had a dark coat on. Between thirty and thirty-five, I'd have said and quite good-looking apart from some scars on his face.' She paused. 'Glasgow accent, I think, or somewhere round about there. Otherwise, that's it. Except ... now I think about it, there was something odd about his face. Not just the scars. There was a change of texture and colour. It was like he'd used that concealer make-up to hide something.'

'Did he touch anything, do you know?'

Honey asked.

'He had gloves on when I saw him.'

Honey kept the talk going, in the form of a conversation rather than an interrogation. She had the impression that Miss Morrison had quite fancied the man but nothing further of any use emerged.

Dorothy and the warden watched interestedly as Honey made a quick search of Harriet Benskin's side of the room. It was obvious that her removal had been complete and probably permanent. What little remained was only fit for disposal, but it would have to be collected and examined. The dead girl's fingerprints would be obtainable from the discarded make-up containers. At first glance these seemed surprisingly unfamiliar to Honey. Then she realised that a black skin would require a totally different range of colours.

She thanked Dorothy for her help. 'I'll send somebody to gather up these odds and ends,' she said. 'I'm afraid they'll have to try to find the man's fingerprints, although from what you say it's a forlorn hope. After that, you can clean the room.' She got to her feet.

'But you can't just rush off like this,' Dorothy protested. 'What's really happened?'

'If we knew that, I wouldn't have to make enquiries. No doubt it will be all over the papers and the telly within a few days.'

At the foot of the stairs, Honey paused. Harriet Benskin had left her room with papers in her hand that had not been in sight when she left the building. She could, of course, have hidden them again about her person, but then again she might not. If she had been trying to leave a message behind, where would be the best hiding place?

The biggest painting in the hall hung by two chains from a very high picture rail. As is common with heavy pictures hung by the back of the frame, it leaned out slightly from the wall. Honey took hold of the frame and pulled it outward for an inch or so. Nothing fell, but when she ran her fingers along the back of the frame she came upon a wide envelope attached to the backing by adhesive tape. It came away easily into her hand. It was not even sealed, but on the envelope were the handwritten words: *Please deliver to the police.* It held a number of sheets of typing paper, closely typed but with manuscript notes added at the beginning and – Honey flipped the pages – the end. 'Is this her handwriting?' Honey asked.

Miss Morrison was lingering at Honey's elbow, making surprised noises. She peered through her glasses. 'It looks very like it.'

'Let's go into your office,' Honey said. 'I want you to put on clean gloves, which I can provide, and initial each page.'

'Yes, of course,' the warden said. Her eyes were bright. Honey felt pleased that she had brought a little excitement into a usually drab life. 'Are they evidence?'

'I haven't the faintest idea,' Honey said.

Eight

There was no panda car immediately available to fetch her, Control advised her with relish. Honey took a taxi, summoned by her mobile phone, back to the office and settled down for a read of the typescript that the missing and certainly dead girl had left behind. Most of it was flawlessly typed and began with a date only two weeks earlier. The first paragraph was handwritten:

I am caught up in something offbeat. It may turn out to have a harmless outcome or I may be heading for trouble. Just in case, I think I should leave a record where it will be found some day. If it turns out to be a storm in a teacup I shall remove and dispose of this, so if anyone finds this more than a few weeks after the above date, please take it to the police.

The text then became typescript.

To help you to understand what follows, I must

tell something about myself. *My name is Cheryl Abernethy.* (Honey sighed. She would have to email Northern Constabulary again, to correct the name.) *This may seem an improbable name for somebody who is of African race, but my family has been in Scotland since 1870 something when my great-grandfather, after the abolition of slavery, came to Scotland as a gardener in the service of a Scottish ship owner. My great-grandfather had earlier taken the name of his owner, as was common practice.*

Skipping two generations, my father did very nicely with a string of corner shops in the general area of Glasgow. A black man was a rarity in those days, but that only made his shops more intriguing. He had taken the trouble to find out and to claim all the discounts allowed in his contracts with suppliers (which very few shopkeepers at the time bothered to do) and in each of his shops a gaggle of housewives dispensed papers and cigarettes every weekend. The shops were very profitable and out of his profits he managed to buy me a good education at a fee-paying school for girls. I remember him as a very jolly man, always free with sweets for the neighbourhood children. He had a remarkable knack of being able to answer any question that I could put to him. His strengths, I think, were to read, listen and observe, to remember whatever struck him as significant and then to fit it all together into his own philosophy. I try to do the same.

We were comfortably established in a neat semi in a tidy street in one of the many small satellite towns in the central belt of Scotland. But in the end my father made the mistake of standing up to a gang that demanded protection money. I still do not believe that they meant to kill him, but he died of the stab wounds anyway. The shops were sold for what I believe was much less than their value as going concerns.

My mother had never had the same advantage of education that my father and I had. It took me some time to realize that she was far from being the brightest button on the card. She had been working as a cleaner at the College of Advanced Technology when my father met her, engaged her as one of his weekend (and later full-time) assistants and married her. She was, and is, I suppose, a jolly sort of person, capable of laughing immoderately at things no sensible person could find funny, which used to set my teeth on edge.

When I left school shortly after my father's death, I had all the necessary exam results for university and my headmaster suggested that I could obtain a place and a hundred per cent grant, but my mother was scathing. 'You don' want mess with that stuff,' she told me firmly. 'Nothing good ever comes of it. I've had to do with a dozen educated bastards, professors the lot of them, and a right miserable lot of buggers they are, not a laugh between the lot of them. And work? *Work themselves into early graves, if you ask me. What you want to do, my girl, is go out and find yourself a bloke. Or more than one. Just don't forget to write down their names for the child support bastards. Get a baby or two and they'll jump you to the top of the housing list and put you on benefit and you'll be able to retire. Not bad for a teenager!'*

If I had persisted, I think that she might have come round about university, but I was not sure of myself at that time. My father would have encouraged me, but my mother had no understanding of a society above street level. With her words for parental guidance, I tackled the world. I had no desire to find myself locked in a world of dirty diapers, noises in the night and the smell of sour milk; nor had I met any young men with whom I felt that it would be a pleasure to indulge in the antics leading into that trap. Even if I had been so inclined, circumstances were against me.

Many different racial strains came out of Africa. I take after the tall and slim style that I believe is Zulu in origin, and with the delicate features approved by Caucasians, though family tradition insisted that we stem from the Suris. Of course, our African tribal origins were by now confused, but my physical appearance is the only respect in which I resemble my mother. It happened that I had been born with a serious facial blemish – a small area of what they call a 'port wine stain' beside my left eye. This might have been operable, I was told, but for the growth, resembling a raspberry, close to the corner of the eye. This had a root that intruded on the optic nerve, so that the dangers of any operation exceeded the possible benefits.

I felt marked. A black girl might have held her head up among her white peers but a black girl with a marked face was just that: marked. Friends were few. The pack mentality led to some bullying at school so that I tended towards an introverted mind, a loner and a reader. Boys only befriended me in the hope of sex and dumped me as soon as that hope was gone – or realized. Not that I was virtuous. If a boy was clean, well behaved and above all careful, I might accept him and did so on perhaps a half dozen occasions, but the result was always the same. I had first bestowed my virginity on a boy who had been scarred by the aftermath of a harelip operation that had been mismanaged. I thought that damaged faces might be something in common but even he had proved inconstant. Thrown back on my own resources, I remained a voracious reader.

I gave up any idea of higher education and enrolled in secretarial school. The course was easy for me. I'm a quick learner with nimble fingers so that word processing, shorthand and bookkeeping presented no problems.

Emerging at last into the real world I was in for a disappointment.

The world of commerce is much less confining than school. At school, there is no escape from bullies, but out in the world a change of job is all that is needed. Friendships were easier to maintain. As things were, I could have spent my spare time socializing with other girls, but I had no taste for that. A disfigurement that attracts secret smiles is not a great encouragement towards a social life. In the workplace I found that employers, who might have been happy to engage me, were deterred by the thought of what their wives would conclude from the presence of a young, black and (apart from one blemish) comely secretary. Heads of typing pools balked at taking on a subordinate who was younger, more attractive and usually better qualified than themselves.

My mother was not pleased to have a daughter who was bringing no more than minimal dole money into the house. In the end, to escape the endless carping, I spread my search for a job ever wider with the help of the newspapers in the public library. Finally, I was driven to accept a post in the administrative department of a printing and packaging firm in another small town a conveniently lengthy bus-ride from home. Convenient from several points of view, the principal one being that I had a useful excuse any time I wished to stay overnight with my only friend, Lorna.

The building was an old and grubby labyrinth

of red brick. The money was not good and I was working far below my capabilities, but I was not too depressed. I worked mainly under the supervision of a small and dapper man by the name of Mr Gruber but known throughout the firm as Groper. I was largely confined to the mailroom but I had made a friend of Lorna by helping out in the offset litho room. Lorna did wonders for my image by teaching me to choose clothes that suited me. Left to myself I might have continued wearing the dark or drab clothes of my schooldays, but Lorna showed me that, away from work, bright, paler colours could set off my looks.

The round of parliamentary elections brought changes. Thanks to Mr Gruber I became involved, although my home was not even in that constituency. Mr Gruber never missed an opportunity for what he considered to be advancement. I was already politically aware and, although I had decided that the difference between the parties was almost entirely in rhetoric, I was curious to find out how the political machine worked, so I allowed myself to be persuaded to help. Mr Gruber obtained credit with the local political establishment by offering my services. For several weeks I sacrificed my spare time to stuff envelopes and post leaflets through letter boxes. Somebody must have decided that I was more willing or more competent than most of the army of other volunteers, because I was trusted with the bookkeeping and the petty cash.

I was not impressed by the calibre of any of the candidates. Ours seemed to me to be, politically, a straw blowing in the wind. It was therefore a surprise when he returned from a vinous dinner and, finding me alone for once in the campaign headquarters, decided that I had volunteered especially for his sensual pleasure. I escaped with a tear in my dress and a broken bra-strap, but I left him with a red face and a nasty bruise in the crotch area. Most men would have considered the honours even and left it at that, but not this one. He tried to suggest to the police that I had a terrorist connection, but it was easily established that I was British born, brought up Church of Scotland and had never even met any Muslims. After I had explained, at some length, that I had grave doubts about the existence of a personal God and that in my view anyone who gave a damn about which if any God their neighbour chose to worship, let alone in what form, has to be off his chump, the police were only too glad to see the back of me. Their responsibilities did not include harassing a black girl for preaching atheism. I dare say they were relieved that I could hardly complain to my MP.

To add insult to injury, although I had made it very clear that I had unvolunteered myself, Mr Gruber persuaded – almost forced – me to type the final accounting of the newly elected MP's election expenses, albeit during office hours. It was high time for change.

My opportunity for advancement, when it came, arrived by a totally unexpected route. I suppose that I was ready for rebellion. My colleagues, with one glaring exception, were friendly if reserved, but it was clear that the firm as a whole regarded my sex, age and colour as a bar against promotion. This illogical prejudice aggravated the state of depression that had long been habitual to me. I suppose that I'm introverted and depressive by nature.

Mr Gruber had been particularly unpleasant that morning although I can't remember now what particular slight it was that set my nerves to jangling. Perhaps it was no more than a look or a sniff. He arrived at work from his bachelor digs every morning on a slightly battered black bicycle that he chained to the rack in the firm's small bike-shed. It was his responsibility, twice a week, to deliver proofs by hand to the firm's largest customer and he was absent one day on this errand when I was sent out for some minor office supplies. The morning rush hour had coincided with heavy rain and, passing the cycle-shed, I noticed that only two machines were in the rack, both of them lady's models and brightly coloured.

Thinking it over, I was sure that I had noticed a similar absence at least once before; and I had a clear recollection of Mr Gruber removing his cycle-clips on arrival that morning. But he was generally supposed to be doing the trip by taxi and – I consulted the petty cash book – was claiming expenses accordingly. It was not a short trip. I kept observation from the only window overlooking the cycle-shed – that of the female toilet – during my lunch-hour and, sure enough, saw him return and put the padlock on his bicycle. From my customary stool at the counter I watched him enter the cubicle that served as his office. I made an excuse to knock and enter and found him taking a sandwich lunch at his desk. This was his almost unvarying habit, but I had just noticed that he was also in the habit of claiming the cost of his lunch at a restaurant near the customer's office.

My contempt continued to build but I took the remainder of the working week to do some further research, to think about my findings, to arrive at some very interesting conclusions and to wrestle with my conscience over what to do about them. On Saturday at noon, as the building was emptying, I bearded Mr Gruber in his den.

At first he was indignant but also scornful. 'You don't know what you're talking about,' he said.

'I'm a qualified bookkeeper,' I pointed out.

'I only use my bike as far as the taxi rank,' he answered. I was nonplussed for a moment but he spoiled the effect by adding, 'And you can't prove different.'

'What about the restaurant where you're

supposed to have lunched twice a week for the last six years – which is as far back as I could go in the books. Will they recognize your face?'

'Who's going to ask them?'

'The boss will, when I've tipped him off.'

'You think he'll take the word of a stupid black bitch against mine?'

I kept my temper but hardened my heart. 'Yes,' I said, 'I think he probably will. You're only a glorified janitor anyway. And these aren't your only fiddles. You went out for special coffee for the director's lunchroom.'

'What has that to do with anything?' But he lost colour.

'You used the firm's credit card and chucked the slip in your waste-paper basket. I have it at home,' I added quickly as he made a move towards me. 'Stocked your own fridge, didn't you? You have three other fiddles that I know of and probably ten that I don't ... so far.'

He looked at me coldly for what seemed to be ten long seconds before making up his mind. 'So you want a cut,' he said at last.

'No.'

'Then what do you want? I could turn a blind eye...'

I hesitated for only an instant but it was an important instant. He could stand up to me – but how? He was vulnerable. He could hardly launch a physical attack in his own office. 'We're not all like you,' I said. 'You've been cheating

90

your own employers for years. I want you out of here. Give me your keys now and bugger off and I'll tell the bosses on Monday morning. That gives you all weekend to get clear, in case you hadn't noticed. Any bloody nonsense and I'll blow the whistle now, this very minute.'

'They wouldn't prosecute,' he said uncertainly.

'You're kidding yourself. Over the years you've taken thousands in fiddled expenses and just plain embezzlement. Could you give it back? Could you hell! Come on, the keys.' When he hesitated, I turned to the door. 'Mr Jensen's still in his office,' I said over my shoulder.

'Wait.' I heard the keys clatter on to his desk.

It was like pushing against an unlatched door. I was unprepared for such a quick collapse, but there must have been other and bigger embezzlements about which I knew nothing and which would come to light if the partners began to look too deeply into the accounts. I had to keep going now. 'I'm going to stand over you while you take your personal things – and nothing else – out of your desk,' I said. 'Then you go and you never come back. Understand?'

His face was acid with resentment but I had him by the balls and he knew it. 'Of course I understand. I'm not bloody stupid. You won't get my job, you know. And one day...'

I ignored the threat. He cleared out his desk in an atmosphere that pulsed with fury. When he had left, still promising revenge at some unspeci-

fied time in the future, I sat down in his chair. My knees were shaking. I was surprised that he had given up so easily, but it was only just dawning on me how his embezzlements had probably stretched far beyond the trivia that I had discovered.

I waited for the building to become hushed. Mr Gruber was probably right. Even if I saved them from the depredations of one man on the fiddle there was no chance for a young, black girl to be promoted into the vacancy. It was unfair, but that was the way of the world and I had learned to live with it.

The fact remained that I was saving them thousands. Literally thousands and many of them.

Using Mr Gruber's keys, I went through the place. I cleaned out the petty cash. In the cashier's office, the safe was secure but the expenses of the authorised car-users had been made up and were waiting in a box-file on his desk. I pocketed them. I took the money subscribed by the lottery syndicate. I found and collected my National Insurance cards and, suddenly wise, those of Mr Gruber. Almost as an afterthought, I took a few sheets of the firm's letterhead. I had no clear picture in my mind of how to use these things but it seemed to me that they would be the tools of the trade to somebody who was prepared to toss away their scruples.

I hesitated before leaving. There was one more

area and one more individual cheating the system. I used the photocopier.

Downstairs again, I separated the money from the envelopes, which I put through the shredder. Then, without a backward glance, I walked out. I was conscious of an unfamiliar sensation. It was not conscience, I decided, nor apprehension, nor even freedom. I finally pinned it down. It was that, for once, I felt quite cheerful.

At home, I took my time. There could be no question of going in to work on the Monday. I packed a case and said my farewells. The other members of my family were sorry to lose both me and the wage packet that I had brought home each week, but they consoled themselves with the thought of one less mouth to feed and a little more space to share between them.

I caught a leisurely Sunday train. It ran through open countryside. It was in no hurry but nor was I. I had never before had the leisure to take a proper look at anything outside of the towns but now I noticed a man on a tractor. Where he had passed, the pattern of the soil was changed and I wondered why. Life, I thought, was rather similar. It was a deep thought and I would liked to develop it but I couldn't think how. Would I change the pattern of anyone's life by my passing, I wondered? And I decided, yes, I bloody well would.

Nine

Honey had managed to read thus far, despite phone calls and visits from colleagues and others, all anxious to enquire after her health and that of the Mighty Midget or to gather information about cases past or present. Having reached the point at which Cheryl Abernethy had decided to head for the hills, getting away from it all, Honey realized that this was an example worth following.

She drove home through darkness relieved by yellow streetlights. The threatened snow had come to nothing, replaced and washed away by a light rain, just as cold. Lights danced in the droplets on her windows. The street of early twentieth-century houses glowed with lights behind curtains, murmuring of home and comfort. It was a desirable neighbourhood. The street was on the edge of Edinburgh so that the Lairds' house backed on to farmland, now wrapped in darkness. There was no sign of Sandy's car.

Honey's first call was in the kitchen, where

she found that Minka was sleeping contentedly. Pippa had been walked, fed and dried.
Honey congratulated June on responsibilities fulfilled. She took over responsibility for
Minka and, leaving June free to cook, she
settled down in the study.

First she looked through Cheryl's unopened mail. All of it was routine advertising
flyers, unaddressed and delivered to any
recipient of mail. She resumed her reading.

*The geographical distance between my
provincial home town and Edinburgh might be
no more than a few score of miles, but in my view
it was far enough. By timing my disappearance
to coincide with that of Mr Gruber I calculated
that, human minds being what they were, if any
watch were to be kept it would be for us as a
couple. If I was careful not to keep company with
any middle-aged white men, I should pass un-
noticed. Although, the chance, as they say, would
be a fine thing. Also my new refuge, Edinburgh,
is a university city with a large and ever-chang-
ing population of students from all ethnic back-
grounds, so that one more black girl would melt
into the background. In the event, remembering
how casual the firm's auditors were, I doubt if
the printing firm will ever be aware that their
losses extended back for many years. In that case,
any hue and cry will be short and desultory.*

I had taken the precaution of phoning ahead to

be sure that the YWPA could give me bed and board. I had no wish to call attention to my comparative affluence by taking a taxi, so I bought a street map from the station bookstall and carried my heavy case halfway across the city. I had been in Edinburgh before on a very few occasions. I was soon off the handsome but rather pompous main streets and into typically Scottish by-ways, mostly lined with tenement flats over shops and service industries. Larger buildings had been fitted in between and the YWPA hostel was one of these.

My place was reserved in the name of Harriet Benskin, which, by happy chance had been the name of a girl whom I particularly disliked at school, thus forming a useful mnemonic. If I came to a bad end, let her get the credit. The newly fledged Miss Benskin was soon settled into a room which, I found, I was to share with another girl. I had no objection to this. I was quite used to sharing with a sister who was untidy and not always very particular and the signs were that I would benefit in both space and hygiene. When I arrived, there was no sign of my room-mate other than a tidy scatter of possessions on some of the flat surfaces. I took over the smaller but empty chest of drawers and identified my own bed by the similarly vacant locker beside it.

It was still only mid-afternoon when I had finished the process of settling in. My feet were

*still weary from the long trek but they were re-
covering. (I was reminded of the TV commercial
of the Spanish dancer pouring the Champagne
over her feet and drinking the man's beer.) I
decided to take a more intimate look at the city.
For all I knew, my room-mate might not be trustworthy, so I transferred anything that I considered valuable or confidential to my shoulder bag
before changing my shoes and setting off.*

   *Guided by my map, I threaded my way
through some picturesque old streets and a stark
new shopping precinct to a public park where I
relaxed as much as I could on a hard bench,
enjoyed a mild winter sun while I thought dispassionately about my future. This seemed to be
a large, blank canvas. I had barely begun to
think of a pattern for it when my thought processes were totally disrupted by an unruly gang
of children drawn to the park by the unexpected-
ly fine weather and determined to play some
game that entailed a great deal of screaming.
Any chance of reassembling my thoughts fled
when I was reminded by an ominous sensation in
the area of my waistband that I had not eaten
anything since breakfast.*

   *I headed back towards the shopping precinct,
where I had seen more than one café open, but by
a different route, which took me past the frontage
of a solid, Victorian building. It was built of a
reddish stone, and looked as though it might at
one time have been one of the more oppressive*

schools or a trade union. The stern look of the frontage nearly put me off.

But on my park bench I had been thinking very seriously for the few seconds spared to me. I still doubted whether there would be any serious attempt at pursuit, and what there was would be aimed at the unfortunate Mr Gruber with myself in the role of dupe. My small hoard would not last for more than a few weeks, but until what fuss there was had died down, I would be unwise to apply for any financial help or to look for any job which would entail producing a National Insurance card. The sort of casual work requiring no stamps would be unattractive and, worse, not remunerative.

A large plate, much newer than the building, announced that here was the headquarters of a local paper. I knew the name, the Edinburgh Piper, *well. It was a prestigious paper, bought and read beyond its notional boundaries and regularly the winner of awards although its circulation lagged behind the other local papers. It had a reputation for investigative journalism and had been first in with several famous scandals. On a sudden impulse I turned in through the glass doors.*

The interior of the building failed to live up to my notion of a newspaper office. The construction was a mixture of solid Victorian and contemporary cheap-and-nasty and the decor was patchy as though the whole place was subject to

98

sudden changes of layout. There seemed to be a typically Sunday paucity of people, yet there was a constant undercurrent of sound.

A large man who looked ex-army or ex-police, possibly both, and was probably a partially promoted doorkeeper, was reigning in solitary state over a long desk laden with papers and other reading matter. He raised bushy eyebrows at me in enquiry and surprise.

'I would like to see somebody,' I said firmly. 'I have a story.'

The man's look said, I'll bet you have, but aloud he said, 'Not a good time, miss. Almost all the editorial staff have left, those that came in on a Sunday.' He looked at the clock on the wall. 'Monday's paper should have gone to press by now.' He looked back at me. I could read his thoughts clearly. The ones that would bear repetition were that my story might be no more than some snotty teenager getting a job in Bootle, but occasionally a real scoop emerged from just such an unpropitious beginning. His head, and more than his head, would be on the block if he let a rival organ be first with a serial killer or an adulterous MP, although the latter, becoming either more commonplace or less discreet, was losing its power to shock. 'Mr McRitchie may still be here. I'll see what I can do.'

I thanked him, which he seemed to take as his due. He picked up one of several phones, keyed a number, spoke respectfully for a few seconds and then listened. Hanging up, he said, 'Mr McRitchie will be free in a few minutes. Through there –' he pointed – 'second door on the left. Don't interrupt him until he speaks to you.'

I followed the direction of the pointing finger. The second door on the left was open into a tall room, apparently half of a former classroom, where a man was hunched over a keyboard and mouse in front of a computer terminal with an unusually large screen. He had sandy hair going thin on top and was wearing a threadbare old sweater and jeans.

Over his shoulder, I recognized a page of newsprint on the screen. I approached closer, my curiosity aroused. Mr McRitchie was adjusting the position of an advertisement. He made a satisfied sound in his throat.

I forgot the doorman's admonition. 'My God!' I said. 'You can't print it like that.'

Mr McRitchie, who had been unaware of my presence, jumped, span round in the swivel chair and looked disbelievingly at me. He was younger than I had expected; perhaps thirty or thirty-two, and his face must have been both handsome and friendly before suffering a broken nose and sundry scars.

He forgot to be annoyed. Comely but facially damaged young black women in critical moods were not part of his routine. 'Like what?' he asked. I pointed. He looked baffled. 'Photograph of the Queen opening the extension to the Cuth-

100

bert Strang Museum? What's wrong with it?'

'Look underneath,' I said shyly.

The headline underneath, referring to the story below, read: WOMAN ON GRAVE CHARGE. He swallowed audibly. 'You were right,' he said. 'My God! Just about sums it up. Our proprietor's a fervent royalist.'

'It wouldn't look so bad if you swapped the two stories over,' I said.

'I'll do the editorial decision-making, thank you very much.' But he exchanged the positions of the two stories, checked to see that there were no more unfortunate juxtapositions and keyed in a code. The screen went blank. 'That'll be in print in a few minutes,' he said. 'Thanks. Now, what can I do for you in return?'

I had entered the building on impulse but I had had time to decide my approach. 'Do you pay for tip-offs?' I asked carefully.

'Not as a general rule,' he said. 'The national dailies do. You have a story?'

'A big one, I think. Can you give me an introduction to somebody on one of the nationals?'

Mr McRitchie's interest sharpened. Evidently I was serious. 'Our editor refuses to get involved in all the complications of paying for tip-offs – separating the wheat from the chaff, weeding out the stories which would have come to us anyway and arguing over the value of a phone call. Most people come running to us anyway with whatever they've got. But there's a way round it. We'll

101

buy a complete article of local interest from a freelance. How would you like to write it yourself?'

I hesitated for a moment. I decided that I was as likely to be ripped off by a national paper as by a local one and Mr McRitchie appeared trustworthy. My mind was made up when I realized that he was looking at me doubtfully, as though wondering whether a girl of my colour could write at all. 'I could do that,' I said. 'But could you keep my name out of it? And my description?'

'We protect our sources. But is the story hot?' he asked. 'Would we need to get it out now? Or would a day or two not matter?

'A day or two wouldn't matter.'

'Can you operate a pc?'

I just stopped myself from saying that I could probably operate one better than he could. 'No problem.'

'Sit down here,' he said. 'I'd better go and check the email before the print run begins, in case war's broken out or some pop star's had a baby. Let's see what you make of it. I shan't be very long.'

He left the room. I settled at the keyboard and began to type. I deleted my first two attempts at an opening paragraph but then my past reading came to my aid. I had a story to tell and the journalistic trick was to grab for the reader's interest with the first words. After that, facts were *what counted. The screen filled and began to scroll upward.*

I was checking through what I'd written when Mr McRitchie came back, apologizing for the delay.

'Has war broken out, then?' I asked.

'Nothing so newsworthy. Let's see how you've got on.' He wheeled another chair over and scrolled to the top of the screen. After reading for no more than a few seconds, he stiffened. I glanced at him and saw that his eyebrows were trying to merge with his hair. 'You're sure of this?'

'Positive,' I said.

'But can you prove it?'

'I think so.' I opened my shoulder bag and took out a small sheaf of papers.

McRitchie frowned. 'This had better be good,' he said. 'He's a prominent man as well as being an MP.'

There was a hollow place where my stomach usually belonged but I put it down to hunger. 'It is good,' I said. 'The election expenses he submitted—'

'They're on open record,' McRitchie interrupted.

'I think you'll find that this is an accurate copy of what's on record,' I said, handing over the first of the papers. 'And here are copies of the printer's invoices for posters, handbills, invitations and tickets. You can see that only a fraction has been declared. It's the same with travelling

and entertainment. It's serious, isn't it?'

'For an MP to falsify his election expenses?' McRitchie said absently, his eyes flicking from one document to the next. 'Very. There was a recent case...' He read through to the end and then sat silent. At last he said, 'I'll speak to the editor in the morning. This will need careful handling but I think I know what he'll say. The story will have to go to the police. They'll play ball. If the story stands up, they'll tip us off just before they make a move. Then we'll print your article, with any necessary amendments, and we'll sell it on to one of the nationals for publication immediately after we've come out with it. You'll get paid for the article and you'll also get half of what we're paid for it. Would you consider that fair?'

I had no idea whether it would be fair or not. I suspected that it was as good a deal as I could get; but if they had to wait for the police, time could slip away. The money in my shoulder bag would not last forever. 'I'd like something up front,' I said. 'An advance. And a good one, or else I'll take it to one of the nationals myself.'

'That could be arranged. What's your name?'

'No cheques,' I said quickly. 'I'm going to be kind of unpopular and I want to leave as few tracks as possible.'

'I understand that. But we still have to call you something.'

I had to think for a moment before I remembered my alias. 'Harriet Benskin,' I said.

'All right, Harriet Benskin.' He glanced at the screen again. 'It needs a little re-arrangement, but you could have a future in journalism. Do you want a job? Young reporters only come to us to get experience before moving on to Fleet Street.'

'I think...' I said slowly, 'I think I'd rather remain a freelance.' The biggest disadvantage of my change of identity, I realized, was my lack of National Insurance cards in that name.

McRitchie nodded understandingly. 'Let's get this story out of the way and we'll see what we can do. Give us time to check the facts. And then ... I won't ask you for an address, but do you have a phone number?'

'Not yet,' I said. 'I'm going to get a mobile.'

'Can you come and see me here on Wednesday? Make it eleven a.m. I'll have a cash advance waiting for you and an agreement to sign.'

'I'll be here,' I said.

I gave the doorman a wink and a thumbs-up as I left. My emotions were jumbled. I was anxious but I was thrilled. Whatever was to come might be a long time coming but it would not be boring.

Ten

The precious period of peace and privacy was depressingly limited. Honey had no complaint as to the manner of the interruption, but home, it seemed, was to be only a little more peaceful than the office. The sound of the front door announced the return of Sandy and jerked her out of the world of Cheryl Abernethy alias Harriet Benskin. Honey was well aware that to treat Sandy's return as a matter of less than momentous importance would be to sow doubts in his mind as to whether he had managed to capture the heart of a woman who he regarded as the epitome of brains, beauty and wealth. (In this, she thought, he had an exaggerated impression of her but she was in no hurry to dispel his delusions.) This period of insecurity would usually result in a resumption of courtship and culminate, if June were at home, in bed. (If she were not, it could happen anywhere.) To this, Honey usually had no objection but the busier she was the less she could afford the time for dalliance.

She kissed Sandy with genuine affection and asked after his day. His case, it appeared, had begun to open up but had then been caught in the doldrums, as can occur in any investigation when the road ahead is unmistakable but the next witness to be interviewed in the only possible sequence turns out to be abroad, in hospital or a congenital liar. 'It's all about the proposed new refinery,' he said. 'There's huge money involved. We've had tips that there's finagling planned but it hasn't happened yet. There are signs and portents, but never anything to put a finger on. It's like swimming in treacle.'

Honey's case, however, was bounding ahead. She gave Sandy a quick summary of developments. 'I'm just reading the statement she left,' she explained. 'I'm beginning to like the girl. She shows up as a victim of depression, but God knows she had enough to be depressed about. She still managed to keep some vestige of a sense of humour. And she's a good witness. She tells it all chronologically, and tells it well. As a matter of fact, if she has a fault it's that of verbosity, but it's a good fault. You never know what detail is going to prove useful, somewhere along the line. Would you like to read it?'

'Give me time to wash and get my jacket off.'

He was back, spruced and bearing two gins and tonic, within five minutes. His shirt was open under a loose sweater. Honey had used the time to fuss over Minka.

'June says that we have a good twenty minutes,' he said.

'I'll go on from where I'd reached. You can have the pages up to there.'

Honey resumed.

I found a small restaurant and ordered a meal of cold meat and salad. I'm determined to look after my figure, this being one of the few potential assets of a black girl in a white society, but I allowed myself a fancy cake to finish off, with a cup of milkless tea.

It was still only mid-evening when I returned to the YWPA, but the day had been both exciting and exhausting. I have to be rested and refreshed before I have the stamina and, to be honest, the courage necessary for making the acquaintance of strangers in the mass – such as other residents in the common rooms or in front of the communal television. I took to my bed, first carefully disposing of my shoulder bag between the bed and the wall. My room-mate was, after all, still unknown to me. Despite the turmoil in my mind, I was soon asleep. Much later, the arrival of the other girl half-woke me, but I pulled a corner of the duvet over my head to shut out the light and was soon lost to the world again.

Later, I became aware of morning sounds and I began to disentangle myself from bedclothes that had somehow become wrapped around my head.

'You must be Harriet,' said a voice. 'I'm Dorothy. Dorothy Hall.'

'How do you do?' I asked politely. I managed to struggle partially clear of the duvet.

The other girl gasped. She was plump, verging on fat, very pale and silver-haired. 'But you're...'

'Black?' I said helpfully. 'I know.'

The other girl blushed hotly. She was, I realized, an albino. 'I wasn't going to say that. I'm not...'

'Prejudiced?' I suggested.

The blush increased. 'Please don't keep...' Her voice trailed away.

'Putting words into your mouth?' I said. 'Finishing your sentences for you?' I was beginning to find the whole conversation rather funny.

Dorothy Hall failed to see any humour in the exchange. 'Exactly,' she said. 'It was just a bit of a...'

'Shock?' I was beginning to wonder how long I could keep the game going.

'A bit unexpected.'

I threw off the duvet and decided to help the other girl out of her embarrassment. 'I could always ask Miss Whatsit to move me, if you'd prefer to have somebody else in with you.'

'No, no, no, no, no,' Dorothy said rapidly. She

109

was still half-dressed. She flopped down on her own bed. 'I don't mind your colour at all,' she said. 'You probably mind it more than I do. In fact...' She studied me for a moment. 'Colour must be a nuisance and it's damned unfair, but mostly you dark-skinned girls have beautiful skins.'

'Except for a little bit, in my case,' I said.

'Well, yes. I wasn't going to mention it. And, you know, you really don't notice it after the first surprise. I think I'd put up with all the disadvantages if I could have your figure. And legs. I don't know, though. My boyfriend's just asked me to move in with him and he might not have been quite so keen if I'd been...'

'Black,' I said.

'Well, yes. So even if I minded, which I don't, it wouldn't matter for very long because I'll be moving out. Probably. I don't know if I should. What do you think?'

'Not having met your boyfriend makes it hard to advise you. If you've already been sleeping together...' I said delicately.

Dorothy was more outspoken. 'The sex is just great,' she said. 'It's like I'm going to inflate and blow away on the wind, blowing bubbles and singing. And he says it's the same for him, though he doesn't get quite so poetic about it. So you think I should go ahead? I'm a secretary with a law firm and he's a lawyer. Well, he's not exactly qualified yet but he'll be a partner one of

110

these days.'

I had an uncomfortable feeling that I was being appointed as a guru. 'Listen, Dorothy—'

'Call me Dotty. Please.'

I decided that I would have no difficulty with that. 'Dotty, then. I can't possibly advise you. I've only just met you and I don't know the man at all. You'll just have to make up your own mind. Try to think whether you'll still be glad to have him around when the sex loses its novelty.'

Dorothy sighed. 'I suppose so. It's very difficult.' She got up and resumed dressing. Some very frivolous underwear vanished beneath a severe business suit. She seated herself at the mirror. 'God, how I hate Mondays! Do you have a job?' she asked over her shoulder.

'Not yet.'

'Can you type?'

'Yes.'

There was a pause. I thought that she was putting in contact lenses. 'I've been making a bit on the side, doing typing for local writers and small businesses, but all this lovey stuff gets in the way rather. There's a short story and a couple of technical articles on the table. Type them up for me and we'll split the fee. Use my computer. How about it?'

'Yes. All right.' I would be needing income and a sound base in the working world.

'Great! I was trying to make the deposit for a house, but if I'm going to shack up with someone

who already has a flat it rather robs the whole thing of its urgency.'

Dorothy turned round on the stool. There had hardly been a pause in her flow of words but her pale eyes were now blue, her silvery hair was brushed and her face was transformed by make-up. From being a half-dressed tart, fit only for the pages of a men's magazine, she was transformed into the image of a crisp and attractive business-woman. She groped on the floor for shoes. 'I must fly. I'll see you this evening. Or tonight. Or possibly tomorrow. It all depends, doesn't it?'

Out of the depths of my inexperience, I said that it probably did.

With two days to fill, I was content to pass the time busily and, I hoped, profitably, in typing (or, more properly, re-typing) the material on Dorothy's table. This mainly comprised tatty scripts, typed on a variety of obsolete typewriters and then corrected, altered and amplified in various coloured inks and some of the worst handwriting that I had ever seen. Despite these handicaps the short story took only half a morning, but the technical articles were another matter, containing as they did many terms with which neither I nor the spellchecker on Dorothy's computer was familiar. By the Tuesday evening, however, after much reference to Dorothy's enor-mous encyclopaedia, I had not only completed the fair copies but had familiarized myself with *the layout of the YWPA. This might have been designed with the intention of confusing the unwary, with rooms opening off other rooms, so that whenever you think that you have reached the end of the line you open another door and you haven't.*

I also made the acquaintance of some of the other residents. I was driven back to my room by sheer boredom and for lack of anything else to do I began to write down the story of my life so far. I suppose that I could already see that my chosen course could lead almost anywhere.

On the Wednesday, as bidden, I presented myself at the offices of the paper. I had expected to see Mr McRitchie again, but instead I was led immediately into a more expensively decorated office with top-of-the-range furniture. The effect was old fashioned but marred by a metal side-table holding another computer, a fax machine and a stack of newsprint.

Two men were already waiting for me. The one who got up from the executive chair behind the mahogany desk introduced himself as the paper's editor-in-chief. He was a portly man in his fifties, clean shaven and balding, in a dark pin-stripe business suit which, because I am inclined to notice details of men's dress, I thought had never been expensive and was showing faint signs of wear.

He in turn introduced the man who had been waiting in one of the two upright, leather-seated chairs in front of the desk as 'Detective Inspector Andrews of the local force.' Andrews was a lean and sallow man with prominent cheekbones and curly hair which was strangely patchy, being grey at the temples, thin on top and shades of brown elsewhere. He was wearing slacks, a golf jacket and a general air of being slightly but deliberately scruffy, as if to be ready at any moment to pass unobserved in any company but the best.

'You understand, Miss – ah – Benskin,' the editor said, 'that we had to bring the police into it prior to publication? We will still buy your article, if the facts check out.'

'I do understand,' I said. 'You're afraid of libel. You want to pass the buck to the police.'

He sniffed loudly. 'I wouldn't have put it quite like that,' he said.

Andrews was looking amused. 'It's the job of the police to investigate such allegations,' he said. He picked up the invoices from a corner of the desk. 'This is all of it?'

'That's the lot,' I said.

'How did you come by these copies?'

'I can't tell you that,' I said firmly. 'Nothing illegal, I assure you.' I hoped that it was true.

'I need a little more than that,' Andrews said. 'There could be no chance of a successful prosecution on the basis of documents printed from a magnetic image which could have been put into a computer by anybody. They'll have to be verified.'

'You're saying that you'll have to call me as a witness?'

'At a later stage, yes. For the moment, we can keep your identity and whereabouts confidential.'

Little though I liked it, I could see the sense in what the detective inspector was saying. 'I used to work for the printers,' I said. 'And I was a helper in the election campaign. That's how I came to see that there were two versions that didn't even fit where they touched.'

Andrews nodded. 'For the moment, the source isn't important so long as the facts can be verified by the printers. The documents speak for themselves. Verification may take time, especially if the printers are disinclined to co-operate. Court orders and search warrants,' he said vaguely. 'In the meantime, I'm more concerned about your safety and being able to put my hand on you when I need you.' He saw a gleam of amusement in my eye and pursed his lips. 'That's just an expression,' he said.

'I hoped so,' I said. 'Why are you concerned about my safety?'

The detective inspector seemed surprised that I had even asked the question. 'He is a prominent man and a very wealthy one. After all, the laws that he is flouting here were designed to prevent a rich man buying his way into power in order to become richer, so society gets upset when it sees a rich man doing just that. As soon as we start to

115

make enquiries, he will sense danger and he'll realize that the witness and informant is crucial to any steps being taken against him. He may have sources of information that we know nothing about. And you would not be difficult to find. Need I say more?'

I began to feel distinctly hollow. 'I suppose not,' I replied. 'If you really think—'

'Put yourself in his position. What would you do?'

Looking at it from that viewpoint, the void in my middle became a vacuum. 'What should I do?' I asked.

'First,' said Andrews, 'take it easy. We have routines for these situations. Witness protection, we call it. As I understand it, you're unemployed?' – I nodded – 'That makes it easier. We can spirit you away for a few days without giving too many explanations. Who has to know?'

A few seconds of thought satisfied me that there was no one. 'I've paid at the YWPA until the end of the month, but maybe I should tell the warden I'll be away for a few days, otherwise I can't think of anyone else who'd give a damn.'

The two men exchanged a look. 'Would you write the warden a note?' asked Andrews. The editor pushed a sheet of paper and a fat ballpoint pen across the desk.

'Couldn't I tell her myself?' I asked. 'I'll need some things from my room.'

Andrews shook his head. 'Segregation starts

116

immediately,' he said. 'If you see her, say as little as possible. It's the only way. If the room's empty we can let you collect what you want. Otherwise a WPC will collect it. Normally, we would hide a witness among crowds; but you may be a little too noticeable for that. Could you cope with country-side?'

'Cows and things? I expect so.' I had had very little acquaintance with the countryside but what little I had seen of it seemed harmless.

'You can cook for yourself? And probably for a bodyguard?'

'No problem. And do I still get paid for the article?'

'Of course,' said the editor. 'I think that Mc-Ritchie promised you an advance, but it might be better if we purchased the article outright. Is this satisfactory?' He pushed another paper across the leather desktop. It turned out to be a receipt for a substantial sum of money in return for all rights to my article. He followed it with a fat envelope containing used ten-pound notes. I counted them and the amount corresponded with the figures on the receipt. It was substantially more than I had dared to expect.

My first reservation – a suspicion that I was being cunningly gypped out of my dues – vanish-ed. But without that comparatively harmless possibility, the set-up seemed to be balanced on a knife-edge between honesty and deviousness. I went on talking for a few minutes, not saying

117

anything in particular but using the names that I had been given and I thought that I could sometimes detect a slightly delayed response, as though they were having to think for a millisecond in case of responding to the wrong name, but the delay was so slight that I decided that I was imagining it. And there was something about the inspector. He was, as I said, scruffy except for his hands, which were clean and carefully manicured. I would have expected the reverse of a detective. Then I told myself that I was reading too much into too little. All the same, I decided to leave some sort of a trail. Not too much, but some.

I stowed the money in my shoulder bag, signed the receipt. I was sent off in the care of a man who had been waiting in some nearby room. They referred to him as Jimmy. He seems very gruff but I think we can get along. It was a blessing that I'd already started to tell my story or I wouldn't have had time. Typing the rest of this while Jimmy thinks I'm packing. Good job I'm quick and Dotty's printer's a quiet one.

(The last paragraph reverted to the hasty scrawl of the first.) *No more time alone. I'll leave this somewhere Jimmy won't see it.*

Eleven

June had already called twice to tell them that their meal was on the table, but Honey had been hurrying to finish the closely typed pages. Sandy, an adept speed-reader, was overtaking her. Now, however, each suddenly succumbed to hunger pangs and to the knowledge that June's patience would be near extinction. Honey plucked up Minka and they hurried into the dining room where Honey dumped the baby into June's arms – an act that always had much the same effect on June as popping a dummy into the mouth of a fractious infant.

When they had embarked on the mushroom and herb soup and had the room to themselves, Honey said, 'I still like the girl, but I like her rather less than I did.'

'Because she's a misery guts?'

'That too. But you can't help your nature and if she was subject to depression, she had that in common with a lot of talented people. You have to have a thick skin to be content in this world. No, it's mostly because

119

she's managed to tell her story without giving away names or places – except for the editor, which may not be a real identity, and the supposed Detective Inspector Andrews who certainly isn't.'

Sandy nodded sympathetically without interfering with the flow of soup. When his plate and mouth were empty, he said, 'The only DI Andrews we have for a colleague is putting on weight and he's rather jolly and rosy-faced. Whether the name Gruber is real or false, a firm of printers that had recently lost a fraudulent member of staff is very unlikely to admit it. Businesses hate admitting to having been defrauded in case it's taken as an example and an invitation. From her point of view, I suppose she had to guard against accidental discovery of her words before she was ready for disclosure. She probably thought that if push came to shove we could probably work out who was who.'

'She may have had too touching a faith. But we'll have to go through the motions,' Honey said. She helped herself to the last piece of thin, crisp toast and reached for butter. 'And these aren't the sort of questions that can be asked over the phone with a realistic chance of an honest answer. We don't even know where to start. One small town, an inconvenient bus-ride from another but not too far from Edinburgh. We can probably take it as being within easy reach of Glasgow by train, but there must be a hundred such in the central belt.'

'They all have different accents,' Sandy said.

'Only in tiny ways. Could you tell a Grangemouth accent from Falkirk?'

'I doubt if we have anybody who could. They'd have more chance of telling Possilpark from Govan. But we didn't hear the girl speak. I don't suppose her room-mate or Miss Whatsit could do more than tell Edinburgh from Glasgow, but we'll have to ask them. You'd better let Strathclyde in on the act and get local officers hunting round, looking for businesses and MPs that fit the parameters.'

'Sensible,' Honey commented. June re-entered the room with a dish of brown trout. 'June,' Honey said, 'could you cope if I went off for a day or two? Look after my two babies? And the dog?'

June sniffed. 'Don't I always?' she said.

'I count as one of the babies, do I?' said Sandy.

'Of course. But only for catering and laundry.'

'I don't get nursed?'

'No. You don't get nursed.'

'You two!' June said. She flounced out of

the room but there was a lift to her voice that said she was not displeased.

In the morning, Honey telephoned until her ear felt overheated by contact with the earpiece. With approval obtained by Mr Blackhouse from the chief constable's office, she set up the enquiries to be made into the identity of the missing girl, made contact with Northern Constabulary and the officer on whose desk the dead girl's photograph had arrived, and cleared her trip with her superiors. After a light lunch she headed the Range Rover northward.

It was a cold, clear day. The winter sun was low and bright but at least it was behind her and only troublesome when it blazed through one of the mirrors. The CD stack was loaded with a mix of ballet and musicals. The roads were dry for once. As soon as she cleared the Edinburgh traffic she was flying. The A9 was relatively uncluttered so that the usual waits for overtaking opportunities at the sections of dual carriageway proved unnecessary. Her route took her between bare slopes of the Monadhliath and the Cairngorm Mountains. She made the run as far as Inverness in a little over two hours without interference from any Traffic cars.

Inverness is beginning to rank with the worst in Britain for traffic and parking, especially for those not familiar with its so-called traffic system. The sun had dipped and driving was at its most difficult, with car lights, perforce on dipped beam, bright enough to dazzle but, paradoxically, not bright enough to light up the road. Suicidal mammals, including human pedestrians, were next to invisible. It would have been a shorter trip to follow the southern shore of the Beauly Firth, but, well aware of the difficulty of driving in Inverness traffic for the comparative stranger, Honey had booked herself into an excellent hotel in Beauly and arranged to meet her contact there. She survived the worst of the traffic, left Inverness behind at the big roundabout and crossed the big suspension bridge. Almost immediately she turned off as if for North Kessock, nestling almost under the bridge. A stranger might have gone the long way round by Tore, but almost immediately after leaving the main road Honey turned off again, into what seemed like an area of housing; from there an almost insignificant road runs along the very shore of the Beauly Firth, furnishing a short cut for those who know it. It brought her to within a few miles of her destination.

Honey found a parking space right outside her hotel. When she came down from her room, washed and freshly made up, she turned into the lounge. The representative of

Northern Constabulary was supposed to be waiting for her there. Several parties of three or four were taking coffee or drinks. There was one man on his own, but he must have been seventy years old if not eighty. That left a rather pudding-faced woman with a black fringe, a large bust and a jacket and skirt of denim.

The woman turned out to be Detective Sergeant Bleeke, 'Please call me Monica'. She had been home for her 'tea' earlier but was quite amenable to following Honey, who had not eaten since her light and early lunch, into the dining room and to accept a cup of tea and a slice of toast.

Honey ordered her usual scampi with a single glass of the house white. Not that she had more than a mild fondness for king prawns, but she felt that this was one of the dishes most difficult to prepare satisfactorily at home. With the order placed, Honey was able to give a fuller account of the case so far. DS Bleeke appeared daunted by being suddenly confronted and outranked by an elegant lady dressed soberly but fashionably in soft tweed, but she seemed to be absorbing the information.

'My boss, Inspector Munro, looked at the photographs,' said the sergeant at the end of Honey's recital. 'He says that you can recognize this area in some of the photographs but there's not much in the photograph of the dead girl – if that's what she is – to show that it was taken around here. On his orders, I came over this afternoon and tried to pin down where the photographs were taken from, but that was no good.' She sighed.

Honey concluded that Monica Bleeke was one of those individuals for whom the effort of using her brain, or even of doing anything at all, was too much. 'We can't do much without daylight,' Honey said. 'I agree that you can't see much through the window in the background, but what you can see, and the window itself, look very much like glimpses that you get in the other photographs. Daylight doesn't last long up here at this time of year. This hotel starts serving breakfast at seven. Meet me outside the North Kessock Hotel at eight thirty and we'll look into it.' It occurred to her that the DS was just the sort of person who would mistake the day, time or place. 'Give me your mobile number.'

Honey finished her meal alone and in peace, fended off the approaches of a predatory male tourist and took to her room. She used her own mobile to call Sandy, as was her invariable habit when sleeping away from home. They exchanged pleasantries. Minka was well and happy. June had grumbled about the amount of laundry she was left to deal with and had then bullied Sandy into changing down to the skin. Pippa had been walked; she had picked up a tick but June had removed it without leaving the head parts behind. Sandy himself was doing well and was just awaiting the arrival of his girlfriend who had promised to come and keep him warm.

That last statement Honey took with a whole barrowload of salt. She was about to respond with a fiction about her own affair with the predatory tourist when Sandy said, 'The warden at the YWPA hostel was trying to reach you. Apparently something's arrived in the post for your Harriet Benskin, AKA Cheryl Abernethy. Addressed personally this time.'

Honey was not expecting to wait around for long enough for mail to catch up with her. 'Do me a favour please, Sandy, and have it picked up, whatever it is. It's probably somebody trying to sell her some double-glazing or next year's hideous garden flowers, but I'll have to look at it. With luck, it could be the next chapter of her auto-biography.'

The call finished with an exchange of endearments that are no concern of ours and Honey settled down to watching a play on television.

Twelve

Honey was sometimes at a loss when duty required her to sleep away from home. In younger days she had been quite accustomed to sleeping, like the proverbial log, in beds other than her own; but she had become addicted to comfort, to family life and to the warmth of his company although she would not have allowed Sandy to know it. Instead, without quite saying so aloud, she usually tried to suggest to him that her time away from home was spent in a round of conviviality.

A totally uninteresting evening on television encouraged her to take to her bed with a book. After the early night she awoke, fully rested, with time in hand and no dog to walk. For once, she could afford to dawdle. She had a leisurely shower, dressed and took breakfast and, when she settled her account and left, her hair and make-up were impeccable. She believed in doing her utmost at her job but she also believed that to present herself to the world in her best possible state was a courtesy that she owed to the world in exchange for her living. Her light travelling luggage would not have allowed for a spare outfit without crushing, but her soft tweeds remained immaculate and she had brought accessories introducing a change of colours from pale moss green to a soft pink. She cleaned her shoes with the materials provided and when she left the hotel she was in a state that she considered fit to show the world.

It was a bright morning but with a brisk and bitter wind cutting across the water from the general direction of Clachnaharry. She spared a minute for a glance around. The small town of Beauly was attractive, perhaps more so since the flow of traffic had been diverted over the new bridge. The remaining walls of the priory stood up, bravely red, out of the grass.

She took the road along the side of the Firth again. The wind was whipping up choppy waves to break on the northern shore but with the tide low they could not reach the road. All the same, Honey was aware of the damage that salt spray could do to her car. The road was single-track with passing places and at commuting time it seemed to be in general use as a short cut so that her progress was not swift, but even so she was ten minutes early at the rendezvous.

The sergeant arrived, very flustered, five minutes late. Honey, whose punctuality was notorious, was unimpressed. Nor was she mollified when offered a seat in a rusty Lada. Instead, she took Sergeant Bleeke into the Range Rover, thereby unintentionally completing that young lady's discomfiture, and they set off back towards Beauly. The Range Rover, which had started at the top of the range, had later, at the command and expense of Mr Potterton-Phipps, been breathed on by experts and fitted with luxuries usually only to be found in stretched limousines and private jet aircraft. Honey's father liked to have a go-anywhere vehicle but nothing would induce him to lower his standards. He worked hard for his comforts and intended to enjoy them.

The DS was clearly aware that she had failed to shine and it was in a small voice that she said, just after they had passed the caravan site, that *this* was where the photographs seemed to have been taken from. She was pointing to the middle of a grassy field.

Honey pulled into one of the passing places and stopped. 'How did you work that out?'

The sergeant fumbled out one of the photographs. As soon as she set eyes on it, Honey knew that the sergeant's morale was due to take another tumble. 'I lined up the boat's mast with that whatever it is on *Cnoc na Moine*. And you can see in the photograph that the tide was high and I had to allow for that.'

Honey tried to exclude both amusement and censure from her voice. 'So you concluded that what was obviously an interior shot was taken in the middle of a field?'

'I thought perhaps a caravan...?'

Honey's overstretched patience gave way. 'If there ever was a caravan with that much space inside I'd have bought one. It didn't occur to you that that's a working boat, fishing or gathering mussels or taking out parties of salmon anglers, and that it could have been moved to a different anchorage since the photograph was taken?'

The other woman flushed and bit her lower lip. 'No, it didn't,' she said at last. 'I'm not used to boats. Colour me stupid.'

At once, Honey felt disarmed by such a frank admission when some officers would have struggled to justify themselves or to pass the blame. She took back the photographs and selected two of them. 'This one's the sharpest,' she said, 'and it seems to agree with what you can make out of the view through the window beyond the dead girl. If you line up the thingummy on the hilltop with that white building instead of the boat, the line hits the shore west of here. I'll drive on. You keep an eye on those two marks. Tell me when they come in line.'

She drove on with the broad estuary on her left. The commuter traffic seemed to be over. When DS Monica Bleeke said, 'That's about it,' there was again a field on the right, but this time a strip of trees and bushes angled up the slope away from the road and the water. It was half hiding a rough track. A roof was showing above a swell of the ground.

Honey parked in the mouth of the track. 'From here we walk,' she said. 'We may want to preserve any tracks. And if there's anybody there, alive, I'd prefer that they didn't drive away until we've had a serious word.' DS Bleeke, who had seemed to be on the point of issuing her senior with a traffic ticket for blocking the lane, nodded and relaxed.

The day had turned bitterly cold. The wind was still gusting off the water. The lane was muddy and there was dark cloud beginning to loom from the south; but Honey had her good sheepskin coat and hat and she knew that her soft suede, calf-high boots were watertight. The DS, evidently trying to keep face with the detective inspector, wore a thin coat and pointed shoes. Honey decided to take pity. She dug out the Wellingtons that were permanently in the back of the Range

Rover and lent the girl her spare Barbour waxproof coat. The boots were a reasonable fit but the coat looked tight across the shoulders and chest. Honey, who sometimes felt that a little more bosom would not have come amiss, was unsympathetic.

The track led uphill towards a cottage, most of which had been hidden from the bottom of the track by an undulation of the field. On a better day it would have been an attractive scene, the unpretentious cottage with its air of comfortable seclusion, set in the fields against a background of evergreens, with its own trees nestled around it. As they came closer they began to recognize features that had appeared in the photographs. In one shot, the girl had been seen seated on the upturned log that stood beside the front door; in another she was leaning against the same doorpost.

'Go ahead and knock,' Honey said. 'You're the local officer.'

DS Bleeke knocked without getting an answer. She tried the door and found it locked. She looked at Honey questioningly, evidently having adopted the more senior lady as a guide, philosopher and friend.

'Now we walk round, looking in at the windows,' Honey said.

They did not have to walk very far. In the photograph that included the dead girl, although the window area was over-exposed and out of focus it had suggested an oblique view across the Firth. The window to one side of the door revealed a dark sitting room without people alive or dead. Honey stood back and let DS Bleeke look through the other front window. She had seen enough corpses for the moment. The ability of this one to shock had been lessened by the photographs. On the other hand, Honey found that the uncertainty of wondering brought a new stress. Was the girl still there? Had she moved? Been removed? A serving police officer, particularly a detective, has to learn detachment but there remains always the atavistic fear of the apparently deceased. In Honey's experience, that dread would vanish as soon as the body was pronounced or found to be incontrovertibly dead.

Monica Bleeke was less trammelled by an active imagination. After a single, horrified squeak, she said, 'There she is. What do we do now? Break in?'

'Better not,' Honey said. Reassured by Monica's obvious certainty that the grim reaper had finished the job, Honey studied the corpse from this fresh angle. The light was poor and her study told her very little. 'She's obviously dead and the SOCOs will want a clear run at it,' Honey said. 'What you do now is to take a look through the other windows, just in case there's somebody else in there who's still in need of help or arrest, and then report in. Where are you based? Headquarters?'

The DS shook her head. 'Burnett Road nick,' she said.

'You'd better report to your immediate boss and ask for instructions. You can say that I'll wait around as a witness until they've got my statement. We may as well wait in the car where it's warm while you do it.'

The sergeant, less experienced in murder enquiries and so less blasé than Honey, seemed slightly shocked by this cavalier approach, but they walked back to the Range Rover together, leaning against the wind. Monica made her call, standing to attention beside the car except for a quick look at the Range Rover's number plate, while Honey ran the engine for long enough to restore a little warmth through the heater.

When the other had settled in the passenger seat, Honey asked, 'What did they say, Monica?' Honey felt that a limited IQ was no more the girl's fault than that she had been promoted in spite of it and that she had better be put at her ease before she was surrounded by superiors who could be expected to be in a snappy mood after the disturbance to their placid routine.

'I'm to wait here, keep the public away and show the place to ... all the usual people, whoever they may be.'

This was ancient history to Honey. 'Police surgeon, pathologist, photographer, SOCOs, detectives,' she said. 'Probably the procurator fiscal.'

'That's all?'

'Usually. Forensics usually wait to have samples brought to them for analysis but you never know, and you sometimes get specialist experts called in even this early. Then later the mortuary wagon. I suggest you get on the radio again and call the local woodentops – I must stop using that expression,' Honey corrected herself. 'It's a habit left over from the Met and even there they don't like it. I mean the uniformed branch. Get the local bobby to come. You, Monica, will be wanted to make or take statements and to dogsbody for absolutely everybody; and you can't do that at the same time as trying to keep control of the parking and chase the nosy parkers and the media away. I've been a detective sergeant myself. And if you're thinking that I'm getting out of my nice warm car to direct passers-by to pass on by, you can put it out of your mind. I'm here as a witness and that's all.'

Monica Bleeke made a sound that was not far removed from a giggle. 'I wouldn't dream of it. But if you're going to call me Monica—'

'No,' Honey interrupted, 'you cannot call me by my nickname.'

'I didn't even know that you had a nickname,' Monica said plaintively. 'I only wanted to know if it was all right to call you Mrs Laird.'

Honey was abashed. 'Thus far and no further,' she said.

The first rain rattled against the car. 'Do you want your coat and boots back now?'

'Keep them on. You'll need them. Get them back to me when you can. I've spares at home.' Honey reached behind her for her laptop computer and plugged its cord into the cigarette lighter socket. Luckily the statement that she had prepared earlier was still in its memory. With spasmodic assistance from Monica Bleeke, she set about amplifying and extending it.

An hour later, the police surgeon had arrived and departed. Monica had had to break a small window to let him in. Now, rather green about the face and ears, she was dancing attendance on the photographer and the pathologist. Three SOCOs were straining at the leash, waiting to be let loose on the crime scene.

Honey was quite accustomed to the pace

of murder enquiries, which tend to start with frenzied activity before slowing right down to allow time for the various experts to plod along their well-worn paths. She moved her Range Rover out of the lane and into a nearby passing place and used her mobile to bring Mr Blackhouse up to date. Then she settled down with a magazine. Nearly another hour had passed before an enormous 4X4 of American construction pulled in behind her. Two men emerged. From their confident demeanour she judged that these were the senior detectives who would be taking over. The younger, a sandy-haired man in what she recognized as a tweed overcoat with a Gore-Tex lining and a waterproof cap with integral earflaps, strode up the track towards the cottage. The other, a heavily built man with a Barbour and an aggressive strut, arrived at the door of the Range Rover. Honey lowered her window.

'Detective Superintendent Largs.'

'Detective Inspector Laird,' Honey replied. She now found herself in an old quandary. A junior officer is expected to stand in the presence of a senior until invited to sit. On the other hand, the ancient custom that a gentleman stands for a lady still remains in vestigial form among old-fashioned officers. If both rules were to be followed between a female junior and a male senior, neither

137

would ever be seated. If any solution had ever been promulgated on the subject, Honey had never seen it, so she had compromised. All else being equal, she would stand up out of respect for any male officer on the second grade above her own. The sole exception was Mr Blackhouse, for whom she had little respect and who had long stopped expecting it. For a female superior, she would stand. But for a male superintendent belonging to a different force who was standing in the wind and rain outside her vehicle, wearing a long waterproof coat of waxed cotton while she had already removed her sheepskin, she decided to stretch the rules of both courtesy and discipline. 'Do please get in out of the rain, superintendent,' she said.

Mr Largs grunted and walked round the car. He hesitated before opening the passenger door, but obviously there was no way for him to get rid of his wet coat and sit down without getting soaked, so with another grunt that she could take for apology if she so wished, he brought the rain with him and shut the weather outside. Honey could see what her father meant about regretting not having insisted on all-leather upholstery. Detective Superintendent Largs looked around the interior of the car, the Sat Nav, the top-of-the-range hi-fi, the leather and the polished woodwork and he grunted for the third time. 'Lothian and Borders seem to look after their inspectors,' he said.

'This,' Honey said, 'is my own car.'

He looked at her in surprise and suspicion. 'Laird,' he said, 'Laird. Of course. I've met your father, Robin Potterton-Phipps. They call you Honeypot, don't they?'

'My father does, sometimes,' Honey said. 'Nobody else still living.'

After a pause he laughed, a deep bark of laughter. 'I'll remember. Now, inspector, tell me about this case.'

'You can read my statement, if you wish,' Honey said. She opened her laptop and booted up the statement that she had prepared. He scanned through it with total concentration. When he looked up, she handed him the doctored set of prints of the photographs. 'The couple seem totally unconnected with the case,' she said, 'so I have removed their faces. If anything occurs to suggest that either of them has any link with the case I can print them again complete with faces.'

He surprised her by saying, 'That seems reasonable.' She had expected him to be a stickler. He returned the photographs to her, retaining only the prints featuring the girl, living and dead. 'I'd like enlargements of these.'

'No problem. I'll email the originals.'

'And send me a printout of your statement.'

'I can email that to your office right now, if you like.'

He sighed. 'I keep forgetting about this modern technology. Go ahead.'

He gave her the address. She connected her mobile phone to the laptop and despatched the statement.

'If there's anything else, I can reach you,' he said. He put his hand on the door handle.

'I can go?' She was amazed. She had expected to be kept hanging around for hours or even days. 'I'm supposed to be still on maternity leave, but HQ can put us in touch. You'll let us have sight of any forensic results? And the path report?'

'Certainly. My regards to Mr Potterton-Phipps.'

'Your sergeant's car is at North Kessock.'

'I'll see that she gets lifted back to it.'

A few seconds later he was stamping through the rain towards the cottage and the corpse. She turned the Range Rover in the mouth of the track and set off back towards Edinburgh, rather relieved to leave the death scene and all the fuss and flap that usually went with it. She encountered a heavy shower that would not make the investigation any easier.

Thirteen

So the black girl had been right to suspect that she might be in danger. Honey's mind was so full of permutations on the known events that she was arriving in the fringe of Perth before she recognized the ache in her midriff as being hunger. She pulled in at the Isle of Skye Hotel and took a bar snack before sweeping onward, along the motorway and over the big bridge.

Daylight was giving way to street lighting as she crossed the ring road and entered Edinburgh. It was hardly worth going into 'the factory' for what little was left of the usual working day, and a call from her mobile had assured her that Sandy had already got Cheryl's mail to be delivered to their home. With luck this would include the rest of the girl's statement, although it would be a great rarity if it were to extend close to the time of her death. Anyway, Honey was supposed to be on leave; and Finance would probably limit her travelling expenses to the amount of the rail fare. If she had travelled by train she would not have been back for hours yet.

She went home with a relatively clear conscience.

All was familiar, warm, dry and homely. Even the Range Rover seemed pleased to be home. Minka seemed happy to see her. Pippa was genuinely ecstatic, fawning around her in a crouch and singing a dog song. June made at least pretence of pleasure, though Honey's return would put an end to her monopoly of all the privileges of surrogate motherhood. As Honey had hoped, there was a white rectangle placed in the geometrical centre of the desk in the study. She would have liked to open the envelope straight away but she was tired, she had been cold and she felt less than fragrant. She took a cup of tea upstairs and enjoyed a shower and a change into fresher and less formal attire. When she came down again, much refreshed, the usual time for their evening meal was only an hour or so distant, so she felt quite justified in pouring herself a medium-sized gin. The only bottle of tonic seemed to have gone flat so she mixed her drink with an assortment of fruity mixers. The result turned out to be delicious but she was sure she'd never quite manage to repeat it.

She had run out of excuses for delay. She

carried Minka off to the study. June's displeasure was marked by a clashing of pans from the kitchen.

If there had been any pleasure of anticipation it had been stretched past breaking point. As she picked up the envelope, she realized that she had been procrastinating because she knew that what was to come could only be a harrowing read. These would be the last words from a girl who had suffered but did not know that she was about to die.

Honey picked up the outer envelope. It had taken very little time for the junk mail marketers to put the girl, under her alias of Harriet Benskin, on their lists. She was invited to buy plants at a garden centre and to attend a symposium on timeshare holiday homes. Below a free sheet of useful local numbers and addresses there was a second envelope, which had been postmarked Inverness, addressed to Harriet Benskin in a familiar hand and endorsed: 'To await collection'. The stamp seemed to have been steamed from some earlier correspondence and glued in place using flour and water, but it had been accepted. Honey, carrying Minka, went for her bag and found a pair of paper gloves. She settled with the baby on her knee and slit the envelope.

Inside were several sheets of typing paper,

closely written on in the same hand and clipped together. But at least, Honey thought, it
was a clear hand, as quick to read as poor
type.

*If all is well, I shall burn this. Or perhaps use it
as the basis of a novel. But whoever gets their
hands on this should know that this is the second
part of the story. Part One is or was in an
envelope taped to the back of the rather bland
and totally mystifying picture in the hallway of
the YWPA hostel in Edinburgh. Read that first if
you can.*

*I had been left in the care of a man they called
'Jimmy'. I still don't know his real name. Given
the circumstances, such caution seems excessive.
He sounds Glaswegian, and every man in Glasgow is addressed as 'Jimmy'. His manner was
noncommittal and unemotional. I had the feeling
that I represented a parcel and he was the postman. I found this disquieting, as if he were a
gaoler, although he didn't keep a close guard on
me. I gained the privacy to finish off Part One of
this biography by insisting, with my tongue
firmly in my cheek, that no man was going to
watch while I packed my more intimate garments. Believe it or not, and to my amazement,
he took this seriously, looking abashed, and
waited out on the landing.*

*Later, I could have run away if I'd wanted to
but I had nowhere to go and I had arrived of my*

own free will. Jimmy carried my meagre luggage out to a Volvo, large and nearly new; it had less than 10,000 miles on the clock. I wasn't given a chance to speak to anybody. As I left the room I gave a carefully anxious glance at the dressing table, where I had deliberately disarranged Dotty's papers slightly. He took the hint and went into the room to check that I hadn't hidden a note among the papers, which gave me time to hide Part One behind the picture. As soon as I settled in the – very comfortable – passenger seat, we were off.

Jimmy was and is a thickset man with, as I have said, a strong Glasgow accent, but like most Glaswegians, if you disregard the occasional slang, he speaks English that is no worse than that of the common man from any other part of Britain – in fact, probably better. He was almost certainly good looking once except for the port wine stain that covers most of one cheek and part of his forehead, though I never saw it until later. I saw him notice the similar stain beside my eye and thought that there was a slight softening of his attitude, though I couldn't guess why. His face looks battered, as if most of the bones had been broken at one time or another, and he has a scar down the unstained side from ear to chin. He is altogether tough looking but, studying his features behind the scars and the stain, I'm sure that he must have been good looking, almost handsome, before he got knocked about. He is neatly but not expensively dressed and looks and smells clean. His luggage, I noticed, was three times mine and took up a large suitcase and a smaller one. There was also a carton of food. He seems to have total self-confidence and yet he's terrified of girls. He told me later that he was brought up in a large family of all sisters with a strict mother and no father. Even the cat, he said, was female. I suppose that that could do it. Followed by a rejection or two, it could certainly have that effect. He handled the big car confidently and I soon managed to ignore the liberties he took with the Highway Code. He was a good enough driver, and familiar with that car, to get away with it. I just hoped that we would not meet up with any other drivers with the same determination to grab the right of way.

We left Edinburgh through Barnton and went over the Road Bridge. When I asked where we were going, he began, 'See you, Hen,' and then he shrugged. 'It's no me joab to tell yeh,' he said, 'jest ta keep ye oot o any hassle, but, man, you've eyes in yer heid.' That was true enough. I've lived my life in a small part of Scotland but I was taught geography at school and the roads are well posted. He seemed to know his way around. We went through a corner of Perth and got on to a road that went on and on, escaping from suburbia and getting into wilder and wilder country, with bits of dual carriageway and big, bald hills. Inverness was somewhere up ahead and the

146

distances to it were getting smaller and smaller.

After an hour on the main road (the A9 it said on the signs) I came to a belated realization that, if I were the victim of an elaborate plot to dispose of me permanently, I had made it foolishly easy for the plotters. A few minutes later, however, he turned off the main road and pulled in to the parking space beside a rural pub. Again, I was reassured. Surely he would neither have bothered to feed me or have allowed us to be seen together so publicly – and in front of the security camera of an adjacent post office – if his intentions were hostile.

The car must have been full of fuel when we set off because I noticed that it was still over the quarter. The daylight was fading and he switched on the car's lights. We brushed past Inverness and crossed another bridge, almost the clone of the Edinburgh one. From the signposts I could see that we were pointed towards the absolute north and if we went too far we'd fall off the edge into what I think would be the Pentland Firth, but only a little way past the bridge he turned off suddenly to the left and turned off again to the right and when we cleared some houses we were running along the shore, almost in the water, with Inverness on the other side of the Firth and the land rising on the right with some fields and a lot of trees.

I had read about the countryside and had even

seen it from the windows of trains and buses. On our way from Edinburgh we had mostly travelled between those big round hills. Now that I was to make its acquaintance at close quarters, I studied the passing scene with greater interest. This was more like the sort of scenery that I had seen from the bus windows nearer home. There was a tranquillity about the fields and hedgerows which pleased me and no animals seemed to be in a hurry to go anywhere. After the bustle of city life and the stresses of the last few days, I thought that I could come to terms with it. Tranquillity shouldn't be boring if you have an active brain. Being of an analytical turn of mind, I looked more deeply into the scenery and thought that I could detect a relationship between the natural features and the pattern superimposed by man, like the printed pattern on well designed clothes. I could not yet understand it, but I knew that it was there.

Jimmy kept referring to some handwritten instructions and a roughly drawn map. We passed one or two scattered houses and a caravan park. Then he swung right and we bumped uphill on a very rough track between trees and a hedge. We came to rest at last in front of a small cottage that, even in dusk and moonlight, looked better kept than its surroundings.

I was halfway relaxed, because it had seemed a long way to bring me if they meant to do me a mischief. I tensed up again, because this might have been a good place for dirty work – he could have knocked me on the head and dumped my weighted body in what I found out later was the Beauly Firth. I looked around for a weapon to use if he came at me with violent intentions, but the log beside the door was too heavy for me to handle and the car's tools must have been locked in the boot.

I was wasting my adrenaline. Perhaps I was being paranoid, fleeing when nobody pursued me. He took the key from a hiding place beside the door and let us in. There were two bedrooms and he gave me the better one, which wasn't even very damp. It seemed that cooking was my responsibility, but that seemed a small price to pay for safety and a cash reward. The bungalow smelt musty, as though it had stood empty for several weeks. I guessed that it was kept for letting in the summer. He made sure that water and electricity were turned on and he turned up the heating.

I had lived my life until then in towns where water came out of the tap, electricity out of the socket and whatever went down the drain vanished magically and forever. With so much around me that was new and strange, I began to take an interest in what made it all tick. From the sound that accompanied any running of the taps, I guessed that the water was pumped from a well.

The bungalow was clean and devoid of

149

personal trappings, which confirmed that it was kept for letting; indeed, the card of a letting agent was pinned up in the kitchen. The bookcase contained mostly books about bird species, so it was a fair guess that the tenants were usually birdwatchers. I had heard that such eccentrics existed. I suppose that it could make an interesting pastime, though the ability to say, 'There goes the lesser spotted doogle-whiffler,' may be overrated. There was no telephone, not even any telephone outlets, so presumably any tenant was expected to have the use of a mobile phone and the single overhead line that arrived via a row of poles must be the electricity supply.

Unpacking, I decided that the box of supplies had been purchased by a woman. A man might have bought the basic foodstuffs but would have been unlikely to have thought of the condiments and would surely have forgotten washing powder. I stowed the perishable food in a fridge that was already cooling down. A wall cupboard contained a small safe with an electronic lock and neatly handwritten instructions for programming the lock to my own choice of combination. I stowed my money in it and set the combination to my date of birth.

Outside, there was a strange smell in the air, which I identified at last as being a combination of wild nature, sea air and an absence of pollution. The constant noise of traffic had been replaced by the occasional sound of a distant car and the cry of what Jimmy said were gulls over-head.

After we had fed and washed up, I was less certain about feeling safe. This time, however, it was not the threat of being disposed of on behalf of the rule-bending MP, but the likelihood of Jimmy thinking he could take advantage of a vulnerable young woman in the middle of nowhere.

I had palmed a sharp vegetable knife from the kitchen and hid it up my sleeve. But we watched a silly programme on a very small TV and I slipped away to bed. There was a lock on the door but no key for it, so I lay for a while with the knife near my hand, only hearing the sound of the telly. Then it was switched off. I was still waiting for Jimmy to come and try his luck when I was suddenly asleep, though I didn't know it.

I slept deeply in my soft, double bed and awoke still alone. From the signs, I had been alone all night and had not rolled on to the knife. The cottage was beginning to seem like home, as though everywhere else was distant memory or even a dream.

Jimmy had been complimentary about my cooking, so I made breakfast. His flattery was not aimed at avoiding his share of domestic duties, because he undertook the washing and tidying. Nor was he incapable of cooking, because later he made a very good Spanish omelette.

He had washed on our arrival and that's when I found out about the port wine stain. He's sensitive about it. There's no reason why other people should be so fascinated by facial disfigurements, but they certainly are. I suppose it's a hangover from primitive superstitions about being marked by God or something. Nor is there any good reason why we sufferers should be sensitive about it, but we are. Jimmy had his covered with concealer make-up but he had washed it off and then he must have found that he hadn't brought any with him. He asked me if I had any. I had to say that I don't use the stuff and if I did it would be the wrong colour for him. I have a similar stain – a haemangioma, the doctors call it – but mine's smaller and there's no point trying to cover it up because of the raspberry-like growth at the edge of it. So that's one thing we have in common, marked faces to attract the stares of the rude and inconsiderate.

Fourteen

A phone call brought Honey back to the present with a jump. This was followed by the homecoming of Sandy, who looked in at the study door. 'This is getting to be a habit,' he said. 'I take it that it's the second instalment of your dusky maiden's story.'

Honey nodded sadly. 'Second and I rather think the last. The story seems to be winding towards its tragic climax. We found her body just about where we expected, in a rental cottage.'

'That's too bad,' Sandy said quietly.

'It certainly is. The super in command, Largs by name, got my statement and then told me to go and bowl my hoop. He's a very rugged-looking man with a scowl that you could use to fry eggs, but I liked him in spite of myself. He promised to keep me advised of any fresh developments. I took that with a pinch of salt, because it's the kind of thing that one says in order to get an unwelcome visitor out of one's hair, but blow me down if I didn't just have a phone call from him.

153

The PM report may not be available for a day or two, but rather than risk losing any DNA evidence the pathologist took some quick swabs. He's of the tentative opinion that she was killed during the sex act.'

There was a tense moment of silence. 'No comment,' Sandy said.

'Very wise of you. Whatever you said would be wrong and I've said it all, from "What a shame!" to "What a way to go!" Mr Largs has identified the owner of the cottage, but it seems to have been rented by nominees and he's still trying to find out who was behind them. In Part Two – this one – she mentions stopping for lunch under the eye of a security camera, so he can try to get hold of the image. Go and freshen up and you can join me.'

She resumed her reading.

The kitchen was small, so that wherever I was in it I found myself looking out of the window. It was a bright, clear morning. The view was partly cut off by a hump in the field but, once I had got used to the absence of people and cars and buildings, it was interesting and just as constantly changing as a city street. When I came to notice it, life was mostly represented by the birds. Without thinking about it or looking very hard, I had assumed that there were, at the most, half a dozen different varieties, but with nothing much else to look at I soon realized that there were many hundreds of birds in twenty or thirty varieties, all with different lifestyles. I began to understand why people might enjoy learning about them.

The water stretched about a mile to the hills on the far side and much further to Inverness away on my left. Over the water, large birds flew, often in formation, like planes doing a fly-past. Nearer, there were smaller birds.

The only food that had been left in the cottage was in a large glass jar half full of peanuts. Outside there was what I took to be a bird table and a hanging wire container. Putting together the bird books and the nuts, the penny dropped at last. I put some bacon scraps and crumbs on the table and filled the wire-mesh thing with nuts and I was hardly back in the kitchen before what seemed to be hundreds of birds were squabbling over the goodies – mostly chaffinches, Jimmy said, but there were tits of all sorts. From one of the bird books I managed to identify several of them.

Some day, I told myself, I would be the mistress of a little house like this, far from the crowds and smoke, and I'd watch the birds and know them all by name. It was the first time I've ever looked at the future with anything like hope. Until now, it has been enough to have survived with my soul more or less intact.

Honey sighed. Sandy, rejoining her in a freshened state, caught the sigh. 'The girl seems to have been approaching a sort of happiness,' Honey explained.

'I understand. It always seems worse when somebody happy gets killed.'

Honey looked at him in surprise. Sandy was not often given to perceptive thoughts about mortality or, if he was, he kept them to himself.

They settled down together and carried on reading.

Jimmy was sitting at the kitchen table, reading a tabloid paper that he had brought with him. The purple stain was turned away from me again. Indoors was totally boring; I came back to my room, the one place where I could be alone. He seemed to accept that a girl needed privacy for doing 'girl things'. I had brought away some plain paper and a good pen and I began to write this instalment of my autobiography. Whether anyone will ever see it I don't know, but writing it down is sort of cathartic and helps me to see myself in something like a true light.

The effort of authorship eventually palled. After all, my life until a month or two ago would have made the average ditchwater look exciting. Small wonder that a state of depression has become so normal to me that I only notice it on those rare occasions when something cheers me up. Then for the past week I have not known whether I was one of the good guys or one of the bad.

When I went downstairs again, Jimmy had moved to a more comfortable chair in the sitting room. I made us a snack lunch and when the washing-up was done I told him that I wanted to go out for a walk.

I quite expected him to object that he was comfortable, that it was cold outside and that I was supposed to be kept safe out of the public. I thought that his main motivation would be that we weren't to be seen together. If he refused, it would be a bad sign. But he looked me up and down and said, 'You'll freeze, dressed like that. Don't you have anything warmer?' In the end, I pulled up a pair of jeans under my skirt and he lent me a duffel coat that did quite well with a belt round my waist and the sleeves rolled up.

Jimmy was quite right. When we got outside and away from the shelter of the cottage, there was a cold wind blowing. Lacking gloves, I rolled down the sleeves of the duffel coat and held the cuffs in my hands. I must have been a funny sight but who was to see me? The only people that I've seen here have been the few who've swept past in cars and one lady who walks two spaniels on leads every afternoon and gives me a shy smile if we meet. It was stimulating, the wind and the wild surroundings, as if we were two quite different people.

157

We walked down to the roadside. There was almost no traffic, but when we met the lady with the spaniels and again when the only vehicle, a plumber's van, went past, Jimmy turned to look over the water. The view was interesting enough, with the sun sparkling on the water and clouds leaving shadows on the distant hills, but not interesting enough to repay so much study. He obviously did not want his face seen, but whether this was vanity or discretion I had no way of knowing.

Jimmy was beginning to talk quite freely. He turned out to be very knowledgeable about country things, especially birds. He told me that, when he was hardly more than a child, he was sometimes sent to stay with an uncle and aunt at Kilcreggan and his uncle had been a source of country lore. The big birds were geese, he said, mostly greylags. He even showed me the differences between several sorts of wild ducks and when we got back to the cottage I looked in the bird books and he was absolutely right. I wouldn't have put him down as a country lover, somehow.

I would have liked to return through the fields, where I thought that there would probably be rabbits, but my only walking shoes would not have been up to a tramp through wet grass. As it turned out, we had to go back by road, the shortest and driest way. While we walked, clouds had been banking up behind us and when we turned round it was to face a blue-black mountain of cloud. Almost immediately, we were struggling into a violent wind and the rain was coming down – I can't think of a comparison that hasn't already been over-used. Let's just say that it was sluicing down.

A duffel coat is comfortably warm but it is far from waterproof. By the time we had gone fifty yards I was soaked through and the duffel coat weighed a ton. Jimmy, who had put on a plastic mac over a fleece, was a little better. There was no shelter along the way, the few trees being leafless. We arrived back at the cottage in a hurry, just as the rain began to lessen.

With surprising chivalry, he insisted that I take first turn in the bathroom. A hot shower restored me to warmth and comfort even though the only towels were small and rough. Expecting a windfall, I had got rid of most of my wardrobe. Now, with my workaday dress and my jeans soaking wet, I was left with a choice between a fancy coat with imitation fur and a thin and clinging dress. I put them both on for the moment, but Jimmy had built up the fire in the sitting room in order to dry clothes over the fire-guard. The room was insufferably hot and I soon got rid of the coat.

Jimmy arrived in a woollen shirt and cavalry twill trousers with his hair tidily brushed. I was sitting on a footstool with my back to the fire, trying to brush out my wet and tangled hair. He took one look in the direction of my underwear, which I had draped over the fireguard and, really and truly, he blushed on the side that didn't have the port wine stain. I had left him some space on the fireguard and he put his more masculine things beside mine, carefully leaving a respectful gap. At least the fireguard now screened much of the scorching heat off me. He gave me his old newspaper to stuff into my shoes.

My hair always dries quickly. I was glad to get off the footstool. He made room on the settee, still keeping his blemish on the side away from me, and I resumed my efforts to untangle my hair. I don't know what came over me. Perhaps it was the domestic intimacy of the moment. 'You know,' I said, 'you don't have to keep turning your left side to me. The port wine stain doesn't spoil your looks. After the first glance you're just as handsome on the right as on the left.'

He made a strangled sort of sound, his blush became almost purple and he dried up completely. I guessed that, because of his port wine stain, he had been shy of girls and had stayed away from them, only going with tarts who wouldn't giggle at his blemish, at least until after they'd been paid. I couldn't blame him for that; I knew the feelings only too well.

When he found his voice, it was evident that I had startled him. His accent became stronger and there were signs of 'the patter' – the Glasgow slang – slipping into his words. 'Ye're a heid-banger,' he said in a choked voice. 'Ye're the wan with the guid looks. Efter half a minute you canna see the wee plook ony mair and then you're a wee smasher, so y'are.'

I couldn't remember anybody paying me a compliment for my looks before, except for one or two boys who were obviously hoping for a special sort of reward. It was my turn to be tongue-tied. There was no suitable reply without repeating what I had already said. So I half-turned and gave him a sisterly little kiss on the cheek before going back to teasing out my hair. He seemed to have lost his voice altogether. In the end, I turned my back to him and said, 'You can finish brushing out my hair if you like.'

I handed my hairbrush back over my shoulder and he almost grabbed it. He worked away in silence and very gently as if he were afraid of hurting me. Even when my hair was smoother and better brushed than ever before, I let him continue. A girl can never have too much of that sort of attention..

Water had got into my watch, which was only a cheap copy anyway, and it had stopped; but I thought that the clock on the mantelpiece was about right and it seemed that the afternoon had slipped away. It was time to begin preparations for an evening meal. I was about to break up the cosy scene, but wondering whether to give him the chance of an easy and more passionate kiss, when he spoke suddenly. 'You dinna waant tae

161

get hooked up wi the likes a me,' he said.

Somebody once told me that the first sign that an affair was becoming real was when the parties started developing a telepathic link and anticipating each other's thoughts. His sudden grasp at my secret impulse made me jump. Instead of bridling and insisting that there was no way that I would consider getting involved with him or anybody like him, I heard myself say, 'Why not?'

'Because I'm bad news, that's why not.'

That was much the answer I expected although the fact that we were still talking and that he was still brushing my hair combined to suggest that the worst of the news was not inevitable. 'One way or the other,' I said, turning to face him, 'I can guess why I'm here. But why are you here?'

'Tae make sure that you're still here when you're wanted.'

'I'll be here,' I said. 'I've nowhere else to go.'

He nodded silently. I got to my feet, then stooped suddenly and kissed him on the lips. He froze for a moment and then grabbed me and pulled me towards him. I was prepared for anything from a return kiss to a violent ravishment or even a spanking, but not for a gentle kiss on my haemangioma. It was a tactful but convincing statement that he found my blemish acceptable. I managed a quick peck on his port wine stain and jumped up and away.

We ate without speaking aloud although count-

162

less messages were flickering silently between us. Neither of us could think how to break the new silence that was strung between us like a cobweb. I decided that a parallel subject might break the ice without breaking the mood. I kept my tone curious rather than anxious. 'How did you get into your line of work?' I asked him.

He shrugged. 'Born into it. When I was a wean, I ran errands for a man. He'd been a professional footballer who didn't make the big time. I found out later that he worked as a runner for bookies an' that like loan sharks. When I left school I became a boxer but I was just one mair who never made the big time. My friend gave me odd jobs. I must have been seen as reliable because I made my way up the ladder. I've been right through the mill, seen all the rackets. Now I work for the boss of all the Glasgow bosses, but I'm a very small fish in a big puddle. I do what I'm told to do, which is whatever he's being paid to get fixed, and just now that means keeping you safe.'

I got up and went to the sink to begin washing up. Over my shoulder I asked, 'Couldn't you just chuck it? Walk out and get a proper job?'

'No,' he said again, so sharply that I jumped. He paused. 'No,' he said again, more softly. 'Once you're in, you soon know too much. Like I said, I'm small fry – but I could still be a gift from God to the law. You see, there's a new kingpin in the underworld and the days of the old Glasgow gangs are coming back. The police are desperate to turn back the clock, but not too far back.'

'They wouldn't really—' I began.

'So they would!' He paused again, for longer, and I could feel the tension in the air. 'I'll say this once. Dinnae you ever tell onythin, assuming you get the chance. There was a time I helped pit a man under a motorway. He'd tried to quit. He was a freen of mine and he begged me for help but if I'd helped him I'd only have gone the same way. There, now! His face still comes back to haunt me. And think of this. How long would it take them to find me, with this stain on my face?'

'You could get a skin graft. Why didn't you?'

'Why didn't you?' he asked me.

'I can't,' I explained. I had finished at the sink. I went through to the sitting room, knowing that he would follow. 'It's not the usual haem...' I struggled to recall the exact word. I had not heard it spoken aloud for years. 'Haemangioma,' I said at last. 'I was told at the hospital that it was inoperable. It has a root and the optic nerve's involved. Now, tell me why you didn't get a graft.'

'I was scared,' he said simply. He joined me on the settee and this time he sat the other side of me so that I was looking at his haemangioma. 'Shit scared. I've had a man come at me with a razor and once a man with a samurai sword and neither of them scared me, or only a little bit, because I kent each time that if I was quick and

164

clever I could get it affa him without getting cut. But a man coming at me with a scalpel gonna cut me up and knowing that I was going to let him, weel, that did frighten me.'

'Yes,' I said. 'I can understand that.'

He turned to face me, only inches away. There was only one small lamp on but I could see the glow in his eyes. 'Yes, I believe you do.'

We kissed after that and did all the things that lovers do. He seemed to enjoy exploring my body and giving me the guided tour of his, and we took a long time over it. I had expected him to be rough but when he decided that the time had come it was as if he had melted into me.

We have had three precious days, and we may have one or two more, walking the shingle and looking at the birds during the day, laughing like children, and making love at night. He makes love so tenderly that I could almost be sure that he means it. Perhaps it's enough that I can believe him to be sincere if I try hard enough. He gave me a gold watch. He has a camera and seemed pleased to take photographs of me.

He is nursing his cellphone, expecting word from his boss. Somewhere, they are deciding whether I live or die. I can see it clearly now. The evidence I gathered, with accounts and receipts showing clearly that he had faked his election expenses, could damage the MP, and it could make it quite impossible for him to push for the oil refinery site. The syndicate or partnership or *whoever's promoting that site uses Jimmy's boss for any strong stuff. My fate may depend on whether the big man would rather earn a fee for getting rid of me or use me for blackmail. If they tell Jimmy to kill me, he must do it. I wouldn't expect or want him to put his life on the line for me and I know that he'll try to make it painless.*

However it goes, I know that this golden interval won't last forever, it never does. Nor should it. I am in a moment of happiness or pleasure, whichever you want to call it. Such intervals can never endure forever any more than a person could live on a diet of honey and wine. I don't mind a whole lot either way. What future is there in this country for a black girl with a badly marked face? Work, sex, babies and death. At least I shall have had a love of my own and escaped for a while from the black depression that followed me for most of my days. I can take that memory with me, still bright and untarnished by time.

He's asleep now and it's the time for the lady to walk her dogs past here. I'll slip out and ask her to post this for me.

Fifteen

For the remainder of the evening, Honey was noticeably subdued. Even nursing Minka, which could usually be counted on to make her broody and contented, failed to raise her mood.

Sandy could hardly have failed to guess what was wrong. He decided to be brisk and bracing rather than invite more melancholy. 'This isn't like you,' he said. 'I thought you'd learned by now to stay detached from the tragedies. In this job, every case has to be a disaster for somebody. Empathizing with the victim only interferes with cool reason. The most you can do is to take comfort from the fact that you may be helping to prevent it happening again. And consoling the bereaved by letting them see retribution in action, even if it is secondary. We're not in the revenge business, no matter what people think. Our job is to keep the villains out of society, even if society does its best to make the job difficult.'

'I do know all that,' Honey said coldly. 'I'm

not entirely an idiot. I know you believe that women think entirely with their emotions.'

'I don't think any such thing,' Sandy protested. 'If you were strictly honest, you'd probably accept that there are certain topics that the average woman and the average man tend to approach from different angles.'

'I can accept that if you can accept that the woman's approach is often the right one.'

'Granted,' said Sandy. 'Provided that we don't start arguing percentages. Let's just say sometimes rather than often.'

Honey looked at him suspiciously before deciding to abandon that argument. 'But I feel that I was getting to know the girl,' she said. 'I was coming to like her. She was being given a glimpse of happiness and now it's over.'

'And she was dying without regretting its passing. Most people who find happiness will move heaven and earth to keep it, which is impossible.' Honey moved to interrupt but he hurried on. 'Either happiness stays or it doesn't, but the much advertised "pursuit of happiness" is self-defeating. If you chase a fly, you'll find that it's quicker than you are, but if you keep still it'll land on you. Your friend Cheryl had come to terms with the fact that it rarely lasts forever. That was her view, rooted in experience,' he amended hastily. 'You and I are the exception that

168

proves the rule. Her writing leaves you in no doubt that she was of a depressive turn of mind. You said that yourself.' Sandy got up to mix drinks. A stiff brandy and anything could be counted on to improve Honey's mood. When he was seated and sipping a Glenmorangie, he said, 'At any given moment there must be in the world say – to pluck a figure out of the air – a million people absolutely miserable. And at the same time there may be another million who are deliriously happy. A month later, many of them may have exchanged moods. You can't grieve for everybody who's sad or rejoice for everybody who's happy. Perhaps a saint might do so, but perhaps not. The most that we can hope to do is to be sympathetic, help when we can and let it be a reminder that tragedy may strike us later but that it hasn't touched us yet. Meanwhile, you can continue your subscriptions to Oxfam and the others and rest contented that you've done what you can to improve the average of human contentment.'

Honey choked. 'I didn't think you knew about that,' she said.

'There's a lot I know that you don't know I know,' Sandy said complacently. 'I asked the bank for a repeat of my last statement and they showed me yours by mistake. I didn't mean to snoop, but your mandates caught my eye. I don't mind, why should I? It's your money and I respect your uses of it. If you felt a desperate need to go out to Africa and throw yourself into famine relief, you'd have to give up your job and I'd have to point out that you do more towards global wellbeing in helping to combat crime here. Last year, didn't you put away a gang who were beating up asylum seekers? So how do you go from here?'

'Slowly,' Honey said. 'The body and the scene are both in the territory of Detective Superintendent Largs, who promises to keep me informed. The girl's recent history, and probably her background, were hereabouts. However, she must have been afraid that what she wrote down might fall into the wrong hands at the wrong time. She's avoided naming names. Except, of course, for Jimmy, but every male creature in Glasgow is addressed as Jimmy until known otherwise. There are one or two others, and any or all of them may turn out to be just as illusory. We don't even know whether the parliamentarian referred to is in Westminster, Edinburgh or Brussels. If we knew the permissible expenses that he'd exceeded, we might be able to work out where his constituency is.'

'How's that?'

'Because the permitted limit is different for

each of them, a lump sum plus so much per registered voter. A candidate for Westminster, for instance, may spend £7,150 plus seven pence per head if his constituency is rural, five pence if it's urban. I've just looked it up on the Internet. The figures are different for Brussels and for Edinburgh. If we knew the number of registered voters, we could work out the constituency. But I guess I'm going to have to do it the hard way.'

'I guess you're right.'

'Do me a favour,' Honey said. 'I'll give you a choice of two. Either take Minka off me or fetch my laptop for me. I want to start composing emails while the subjects are still more or less clear in my mind.'

Sandy thought about it. 'Hand her over,' he said.

Honey was absent for longer than was needed to fetch a laptop computer. She returned to find her husband sound asleep in his chair and her daughter trying to roll off his knee on to the carpet. She woke Sandy by lifting Minka and depositing her gently back on his stomach. 'I faxed a copy of the girl's second epistle to Detective Superintendent Largs. She can't have come from around the Forth or anywhere near serious water,' she said. 'Otherwise, she'd have known about geese.'

Sandy stretched and yawned. 'All the

same, you'd better not proceed on that assumption. People can be amazingly blind to things outside their experience and some of them never look upwards at all.'

'True. I want to know the identity and whereabouts of a man originating in the Glasgow area, who has a port wine stain over much of the right half of his face and tries to cover it up with concealer make-up.' She was typing rapidly as she spoke. 'May be driving a Volvo.'

'Copy it to your Mr Largs,' Sandy said. 'In fact, you'd better phone his office and make sure that he isn't sending a similar message. There are few things more irritating than receiving the same enquiry from several sources.'

'Good point.' Honey made a note. 'Would there be any objection to circulating other nearby forces to say that we would be interested in hearing about any MPs who are suspected of overspending on their election expenses?'

'Not,' Sandy said, 'if you don't mind bringing down on your own head the wrath of everybody from God upwards. Throwing extra money behind a candidate is the first step towards getting your own tame MP into Parliament. That's why there are rules on the subject. So the elected members get a bit twitchy on the subject. Anyway, that subject falls within the province of the Fraud Squad. You could route an enquiry through them.'

'I'll think about it. I may get an email off before I go to bed.' Honey knew only too well that one certain route to insomnia was to go to bed leaving a decision still to be made. 'How's your own case doing?'

Sandy glanced down at his infant daughter and put his hands over her ears. 'Bloody awful,' he said. 'We know who we should be talking with, but the beggar seems to have vanished off the face of the earth.'

'Literally?'

'It seems possible. This monkey's deeply asleep. Let June put her down and we may be able to get an early night.'

DCI Truss of the Fraud Squad was in his office and ready to meet with Honey. He was a tubby and cheerful man nearing retirement age but still with a reputation for skilled and unbiased prosecution of those who stepped outside the law.

He listened with care to Honey's words and it was immediately evident that he had grasped every implication. 'There was re-markably little mud-slinging on that topic, last time around,' he said cheerfully. 'That may only mean that traces were covered with more than usual skill. But you haven't given me a very good pointer. An MP, we don't know to which parliament, who may or may not be proprietor of a local paper and may or may not be a fervent royalist, depending on whether you choose to believe a deceased witness who has admitted to being a thief and who was quoting from equally doubtful sources.'

Honey prepared to get up. 'I'm sorry if you think I've wasted your time,' she began.

'Not a bit of it,' DCI Truss said jovially. 'Many of our successful prosecutions began with less. We'll certainly check as to whether the more likely local paper employs editorial staff with the names quoted. In view of your Miss Abernethy's reluctance to reveal real names – I suppose Abernethy is genuine? – I'll be surprised if we turn up anything there. There are some tenuous geographic clues that we'll try to follow up. Stay in touch. Leave me photocopies of the girl's two statements and let me know if you turn up anything else. I'll keep you posted.'

Honey thanked him and returned to the room that she shared with three male colleagues. The room looked strange but she decided that this was because she had hardly been inside it for several months. She prepared a detailed report for the two detective superintendents, Largs and Blackhouse. Then she despatched her enquiry to Strathclyde Police, seeking the identity of a man of

Glasgow extraction, a very tough former boxer whose face was both marked by scars and disfigured by a large port wine stain that he habitually tried to conceal with make-up.

She was in the Range Rover again and on the way to the office next morning when her mobile phone in the hands-free mounting played its tune. She answered and received an instruction originating from Mr Blackhouse to get out to Turnhouse airport and collect Detective Superintendent Largs who would be coming off the Inverness plane. She was to bring him to a room, the number of which she recognized as pertaining to Mr Blackhouse himself.

As she drove out towards Turnhouse, Honey wondered why the two detective superintendents thought it necessary to meet face to face when they had all the resources of the Internet, telephones, fax machines and other technological novelties for the purpose. Truly the ways of senior policemen were strange indeed.

Mr Largs's plane was due, but Honey wasted a minute or two in finding a slot in the car park. Much more time could go down the drain, she knew, in trying to convince some jobsworth that she was a police officer on duty. The plane had picked up a tail wind and arrived slightly early, so the monitors in the hall informed her, but the big man was only just emerging from Arrivals.

He greeted her as an old friend and they walked out to the Range Rover together. 'I'd hoped for a car to be sent for me,' he said, 'but I wouldn't have dared hope for a detective inspector – and a very beautiful one, if I may say so – in her own luxury vehicle. This must be important.'

Honey looked at him out of the corner of her eye as she drove, but the compliment did not seem to be the precursor to a pass. 'You don't know what it's about either?'

'I was just invited, peremptorily, to attend a discussion that might be very much to my advantage. Believe it or not, I was also told that Strathclyde would pick up the travel bill. Otherwise I would have had a Traffic car take me to Perth and ask for one of yours to meet me there. But of course Strathclyde have a much bigger budget that either of our forces, though they don't often splash it around.'

'Stranger things have happened,' Honey said. She braked sharply as a white van overtook her and cut in. She began to reach for her radio but then decided to let the other driver get away with it just this once. 'Not very often,' she said, 'but I have heard of them.'

Detective Superintendent Largs was still

chuckling as Honey pulled into the only spare slot outside the main door of the Fettes Avenue HQ of Lothian and Borders Police.

Sixteen

Space comes expensive in modern buildings, but the rooms given over to senior policemen may seem to be surprisingly generous in size. This is to allow smaller meetings and round-table discussions to take place without the need to transfer to a conference room.

When Mr Largs signalled her to precede him, Honey thought at first that she must have brought him to the wrong room. The considerable area of carpet was of the familiar colour but a complete stranger was seated in the place of honour behind the big desk. Too quickly for the thought to be verbalized, she wondered if Mr Blackhouse's sins had found him out. Perhaps he had died in the night or come down with something painful and incurable. But fate had not smiled on her. She saw the man himself, sitting to one side of the desk and looking singularly out of place. To judge from the neat, unopened files and briefcases she could assume that the company was only just assembling.

The stranger was tall, lean and well dressed. He switched on the tape recorder that always stood ready on the desk and stood politely as they entered. 'Detective Chief Superintendent Halliday, Strathclyde,' he said briefly, seating himself. He beckoned Honey and Mr Largs to seats at the table. 'Inspector Laird now has the most complete all-round acquaintance. Perhaps she would perform introductions for the record.'

Honey had a definite sensation of having been tossed in at the deep end, but she collected her scattered wits. 'I am Detective Inspector Laird, Lothian and Borders. On my left is Detective Superintendent Blackhouse, also of Lothian and Borders. Mr Halliday has just introduced himself. Opposite is Detective Superintendent Largs, Northern Constabulary. And next to me is Detective Chief Inspector Laird of Lothian and Borders.'

'Another Laird?' said Mr Largs. 'Any relation?'

'He is my husband,' Honey said. 'And I may add that I had no idea that he would be here. Or why.'

'You are about to find out why,' said Halliday. He had a bland and expressionless face. His accent was educated and was tinged with faint traces of Glasgow. 'There seems to be a strong link between the case of the murder of Cheryl Abernethy, alias Harriet Benskin, and the case that Chief Inspector Laird and I have been working on. Inspector Laird – I'll refer to her as Mrs Laird, to avoid any danger of confusion – Mrs Laird faxed a request to Strathclyde, asking the identity and present whereabouts of a man known as Jimmy. In view of his description and occupation, and more particularly the stain on his face and his sensitivity on the subject, he was easy to pin down as Dougal Walsh. His present whereabouts are not yet known. We'll come back to him in a minute. For the moment, let's just say that at the mention of him a whole carillon started ringing. I phoned Mr Blackhouse immediately and he wired me copies of Mrs Laird's very thorough reports.' He directed a fleeting smile in Honey's direction.

The room seemed a little less claustrophobic. 'Thank you,' Honey said softly.

Halliday nodded. 'Before we discuss the other case, could I be brought up to date, please, on what steps have been taken to identify the characters in the Abernethy case?'

Honey looked at Mr Blackhouse, who nodded to her. 'The body turned up in the territory of Northern,' she said, 'so I've been trying to limit myself to suggesting possible actions to Mr Largs.'

'Which my team is following up diligently,' said Mr Largs. 'My team is busily enquiring of fee-paying girls' schools for a former pupil named Cheryl Abernethy or otherwise, with the facial blemish described. We have asked other forces to do the same. The school's records may produce a town of origin. The cottage belongs to a lady in Inverness and is in the hands of the agents Scott and Haliburton. It was rented over the phone by a man giving a false name and address and the rent was paid in cash by an individual who visited their office, so there may never be any more information there. It smacks of a carefully contrived dead end.

'We have traced the hotel where the couple stopped for lunch. The dead girl's writing referred to a CCTV camera on a nearby post office, but it turns out that the camera was not operating that day.

'The results of the full PM should be available tonight or tomorrow morning and you'll have it as soon as I do. I don't expect it to be very revealing. So far, Forensics has turned up fingerprints confirming the presence of Dougal Walsh at the cottage and DNA that we can presume to be his. The knife is a commonplace hunting knife of a design that can be bought almost anywhere, but it had been honed to razor sharpness. A cast and photographs of it have been sent to your pathologist for comparison with the wounds that killed Jem Tanar.

'Our enquiries are ongoing. The lady with the spaniels has been identified and is being asked about her last encounter with the dead girl. I'll circulate a fuller report in a few days, when I can draw it all together. For the moment, that's about all that I can offer.' Superintendent Largs sat back in his chair and waited for others to do their party pieces.

He looked at Mr Blackhouse, who said, 'There can be little doubt which local newspaper the girl referred to. It has been visited. The staff denies having a McRitchie among them or anybody resembling the girl's description of him. There is no single proprietor, according to the company's register. It's a limited company.'

He looked in turn at Honey. Honey said, 'If everybody has seen copies of my reports, I can't add anything. Except that the local officers in Haddington should be asked to keep an eye open for Dougal Walsh. The postlady told me that the memory card had been dropped into a post box in Haddington.'

'You can take that on, inspector,' said Mr Blackhouse.

Halliday was frowning. 'One matter needs

more work and the area, Blackhouse, is again yours. The newspaper. Unless the girl was hopelessly confused and confusing, part of the truth lies there and the personnel are covering up. Why? Who is the real proprietor? How did they manage to cover up so quickly?'

Honey could see it coming. She tried very hard to be invisible, a trick that she had always aspired to but never achieved. Mr Blackhouse's eyes settled on her. 'Mrs Laird will look into that aspect,' he said.

She had always known when Sandy was amused without seeing, hearing or touching him. The means, she thought, could only be telepathic. He could see that she was being saddled with a task that would be onerous, drawn-out and, in the end, worse than thankless. He was also sympathetic. 'I seem to have a foot in each camp,' he said. 'Until we have some more answers there won't be much else for me to do. I can give Mrs Laird a hand.'

Mr Blackhouse nodded.

'That's agreed, then,' said Mr Halliday. 'Now we come to the other side of the story. Jimmy – Dougal Walsh – was correct. The Glasgow gangs are rising again and co-ordinating. We're pulling out all the stops, but this time the mastermind is playing it carefully. If anything is ever written down, it

183

is burned or shredded immediately afterwards. The organization works with ruthless military precision and discipline. Anybody who steps outside its boundaries is ruthlessly put down, but we have identified the person who is either the kingpin or possibly the kingpin's right-hand man. This, of course, falls within my territory. We were looking into it when we had a piece of luck. A solicitor was arrested for dipping into his clients' funds. We had had some dealings with him previously. He demanded an interview with me and he made me a proposition. He knew about a very much larger fraud that was being set up. He could put back the money from his own fraud – how, I was careful not to ask – and give us details of the bigger fraud if we could go easier on him, and in particular wait until he'd made restitution before prosecuting.'

For a moment the chief superintendent's face showed a trace of annoyance. 'When push came to shove, he knew a great deal less than he'd led us to believe. He'd picked up on some hints dropped by a fellow solicitor who didn't really know much anyway. On enquiry, there seemed to be something in it. Rumours were rife. It centred on the site for a new oil refinery to take some of the pressure off Grangemouth. For some reason it has been assumed that it would be located on the West Coast, relieving the Forth of some of the traffic and taking care of imported transatlantic oil. This explains how it comes to have been dropped into my lap and stayed there. Also, there is some involvement of the Glasgow kingpin – who is of Polish extraction, by the way, and named Ravitski. He gets called on whenever muscle is required. He also provides a confidential messenger service.

'The first break that we got came when a Glasgow tart fell out with Dougal Walsh.' Mr Halliday's lip curled. 'I suppose his cheque bounced or some such thing. That bears out what the Abernethy girl wrote about him, by the way. The tart moaned to the first vice squad officer to speak to her. Walsh had been with the tart – actually engaged in congress, I believe – when his mobile phone rang. He answered it – without disengaging from the girl or even checking his motions, I gather,' Mr Halliday said with a cautious glance at Honey. 'She couldn't hear the whole message but she was sure of the words "refinery" and "got an option on the site". The call finished with Walsh saying, "I'll tell him". Clearly he was being used as a message-bearer.

'There was no point asking for phone-tap authorization. Cellphones don't lend themselves to it and in this day and age, when

Nokia churns the phones out by the thousand and sells them for peanuts, comparatively speaking, somebody like Walsh can have a different phone and a different number as often as his employer cares to pay for it. I set up a whole team to keep tabs on Walsh, complete with listening devices and parabolic reflectors, but – wouldn't you know it? – he disappeared before we could latch on to him.

'We can see now that we should have spread the net wider; we were just too fixated on the west coast. But it's easy to see now that the Forth area makes more sense, being close to Grangemouth, the services and transport and experienced manpower. So it seems that Walsh was sent to stay in or near Edinburgh, where he could easily make contact with the parties. I expect that telephone traffic has been changed to personal briefings.

'There's another task for your team, Blackhouse. If options to purchase land for the refinery are in hand, there must have been at least a promise of outline planning permission.'

'Leave it with us,' Detective Superintendent Blackhouse said helpfully. Honey knew only too well what that meant.

'One last point,' Halliday said. 'I asked for this face-to-face meeting, with the minimum number of persons present, because any leaks could undo the whole investigation. Ravitski is making as sure as he possibly can that we know nothing of what he's doing. If he finds out what we know and what we're doing about it, he'll shut down, for the moment. And I don't want any temporary shutdowns and having to start again.' His bland face changed and suddenly Honey could see the strength that had earned him his rank. 'I want to smash his organization before it builds up its strength and I want to put away the conspirators.

'One officer reported an oblique approach, offering money in return for a pipeline into police communications. The kind of money on offer was such that somebody may be tempted – and not just in my territory. I suggest that we put only the most guarded words into the official domain for the moment and meet again in a week, or sooner if needed.'

'Sir,' Honey said, 'I would like to be clear about this. I shall need to contact Haddington to ask about the whereabouts of a man of Dougal Walsh's description. May I do that by phone or email or do I have to go chasing through there?'

'I suggest that you phone and tell a senior officer to come in here. That principle applies to other questions.' Halliday paused frowning. 'I can quite see that communication entirely by courier and face-to-face meetings may be cumbersome. But our mobile numbers may already have been compromised. I suggest that we buy three new, inexpensive cellphones with new numbers, in the names of three persons unlikely to be looked on as significant – but trustworthy, of course. Then one of us from each team holds one, for urgent messages only.'

'That seems very sensible,' Mr Blackhouse said. 'The time taken by the others to suss out the new numbers may tell us a lot.'

Mr Halliday looked so thunderous that even Blackhouse quailed a little. 'If they suss out the numbers we'll know that somebody in this small group doesn't play by the rules. I suggest that the tape of this discussion goes into a safe and stays there until this case is finished, or at least wide open. Personnel working on individual murder cases should be limited to matters concerning those cases. The background of corruption surrounding the proposed refinery remains confidential. Any other personnel called on to assist on the overall investigation must be impressed with the need for confidentiality and the rules of communication.'

There was a solemn nodding around the table. Honey thought that the job had suddenly gone from difficult to impossible.

Seventeen

With a new impetus given to the two cases of murder by stabbing, Honey would have preferred to throw herself wholeheartedly into her new tasks, but police work can never be so tightly compartmentalized. Earlier cases throw up the need for action; other officers have questions; facts have to be reported or recorded. The rest of the afternoon had to be given over to a clearing of desks.

That evening, Honey would have opened up the discussion process but Sandy had suffered similar distractions and he was showing signs of exhaustion. He begged for a respite. 'We don't live to work,' he said. 'We work to live. I have always known you for a workaholic and I admired you for it just as long as you didn't drag me along with you. I prefer to work steadily and to arrive surely. You're the hare and I'm the tortoise. For now, I have done enough for one day, perhaps even for one week. So, let's relax, sip a little strong drink, enjoy the company of our firstborn if June will lend her to us, comfort each other and gird our loins for tomorrow.'

'A good programme,' Honey said. 'But I was only going to make a single suggestion. One of the big, unanswered questions is the identity of the proprietors or shareholders in the *Edinburgh Piper*, who may or may not be the same as the negotiators for the site. Who do we know who has a finger in every financial pie and who has only to ask a question in the area of high finance to have a dozen gofers answering it or dashing about looking for the answer?'

Sandy sighed. Clearly he was not going to be allowed to relax just yet. 'Your father?'

'That,' Honey said, 'is just who. The weekend that will shortly be rushing at us will also be rushing at him, but we could save at least a day if we got hold of him now and had him sending his sources galloping off in all directions – but discreetly. I have a sixty–forty chance of catching him at home in the evening, but if I leave it until tomorrow I'll find myself chasing him from office to office and leaving messages for him to call me back. And although he's unusually meticulous about calling back, when he does call back my phone's busy or I'm in with the Big Chief. The only thing is that we've been told not to use the phone.'

'True. But how would anyone know that you'd be drawn into the top level of this particular case? They can't be maintaining a permanent tap on the private phone of every police officer.'

'It's your phone too,' she pointed out.

'Good point!' Sandy thought it over. 'I am absolutely certain that nobody could connect me with the case,' he said. 'I have only been doing background, clerical work. But use your mobile, just in case.'

'My mobile's in my bag.' The two were fitted snugly together in one of the deep, broad armchairs that had once belonged in some gentlemen's club. The gentlemen, Honey had once remarked, must have had arses like elephants. Sandy replied that perhaps the passing of the steatopygic generation was why the club had disposed of the chairs. He reached out a long leg and managed to hook Honey's shoulder bag by its strap from the settee with his toe.

Honey found her father at home and free to talk. Some minutes were taken up with an exchange of family news with particular reference to the Mighty Midget. When she could force an opening she said, 'Dad, we have a case involving Big Business and there's no door open to us – except possibly yourself. As usual, can we keep this confidential?'

'Of course.'

'You know about the proposed oil refinery?'

191

'Yes.'

Her father was not usually so terse. Honey made a mental note. 'You don't...?'

'Have a finger in that particular pie? Certainly not.'

'We have reason to believe that there's some chicanery planned. It's very, very important that nobody knows where this enquiry originated.'

'I understand. I was offered the chance to invest but I heard a whisper that all was not as well as one could wish.'

'Any names?'

'I'm afraid not.'

'One thing I've learned from you,' Honey said, 'is that the real owner is not always the registered owner. We shall be making the usual enquiries, but what we want to know is who are the real owners.'

'Of?'

'The *Edinburgh Piper*. Then there's the site for the new refinery. There's been no public announcement that the site has been decided, but it seems that an option is being bought. Who's the buyer and who is the seller?'

She heard her father grunt. 'The first is easy, the second may prove extremely difficult. What about planning consent?' he asked. 'That will be easier for you to discover.'

192

'We'll certainly be asking the local authorities. But the relevant planning department, whichever it is, may not even have been approached yet. You know how these things go. A promise from each of the individuals with real clout...'

'I'll ask my many ears and listen to their voices,' her father promised. Honey knew that those words were almost a guarantee of news. Mr Potterton-Phipps had a major shareholding, if not outright ownership, of a number of firms, each of which had staff devoted to keeping one or more ears to the ground. In Big Business, advance warning may be money in the bank.

When the call finished, Honey turned to her husband. But Sandy held up his hand. 'No,' he said. 'We'll discuss it in the morning. I don't want to lie awake half the night, turning over all the possibilities in my mind.'

Honey said that she quite understood. She then lay awake for half the night, turning over the possibilities.

The next day was June's day for doing the week's shopping, so Honey left the Range Rover for her use. The Range Rover was rather too good for the housekeeper's use and, being tuned by specialists during Mr Potterton-Phipps's tenure, was rather too powerful for one of June's limited experience, but Sandy's male pride would have rebelled at the implication that his car was of lesser quality or more easily driven than that of his wife and he could always draw on the fact that the Range Rover had automatic gears. They travelled to the office in his Vectra. The fifteen-minute journey through rush-hour traffic was time enough for a quick discussion.

She spent a wholly inadequate hour at her desk. A phone call established that Chief Inspector Jowett from Haddington would come in to headquarters in the early afternoon. Meanwhile, a fat envelope had arrived by courier from Inverness. She distributed their copies to Sandy and Mr Blackhouse before examining her own. The information conveyed was scanty. Apart from the evidence of sexual activity and the fact that the knife had unerringly found the heart, the post mortem examination had produced nothing that would not have been expected of any young woman, who had died of a stab wound. The forensic report, as far as it went, was voluminous, but on a quick flip-through added little. The DNA and fingerprints of two people, one of them the deceased, were all through the cottage. The fingerprints on the knife did not belong to the dead girl. Much had been learned about the couple's diet and personal habits, but frankly, Honey

194

thought, who cared? If somebody were pushed under a train, a habit of bum scratching was unlikely to contribute towards the eventual explanation.

Another report had arrived from the local forensics team. The knife that had killed Jem Tanar had differed from the other in no discernible way and might have been the same or at least bought from the same outlet. Fingerprints from throughout the flat were being sent to Strathclyde and to Northern. Honey laid both reports aside in a secure cabinet for later and more detailed study.

Sandy arrived at her door accompanied by a plain-clothes constable. In the car park, they met one of the solicitors employed by Lothian and Borders Police. The solicitor, a small and hollow-chested young man by name of Hogwood, had a Mercedes that was roomier than the Vectra, so they travelled in it to the office of the *Edinburgh Piper.*

They had high hopes of catching the staff of the newspaper wrong-footed. As Honey pointed out, the existence of the two statements by the dead young woman should be a secret known only to a very small coterie of police. The staff of the newspaper should therefore believe themselves to be unsuspected.

The newspaper office showed no signs of guilty secrets. It was possible that the wicked were fleeing when no man pursued them. Or there was a leak somewhere. Or, she thought, somebody was being excessively careful. Or quite possibly the girl had been misleading them. She could almost have believed that the young woman had been referring to some other paper, but the building was exactly as she had described it and enquiries seemed to have eliminated all the others.

The receptionist was adamant; there was no Mr McRitchie employed by the paper. The receptionist was a large woman, nearer to forty than thirty in Honey's opinion, with a forceful cast of features and a very firm manner. She had, she said, been in her post for years, and she said it with a steely look that dared anybody to contradict her. She was the sort of person, in Honey's view, who would not have languished for long in a humble role, but would have risen through the ranks of almost any organization. Honey suspected that she was an executive, a senior PA or possibly a personnel manager, who had taken over from the receptionist for the duration of any crisis. But there was not one iota of proof of any such substitution.

The editor-in-chief, Mr Barclay, never saw anybody without an appointment. No, not even the police. It took several minutes and as many threats of legal action before she would even let Mr Barclay know of their presence. The constable remained in the hall to take note if she issued any warnings to other staff.

Mr Barclay was bald and clean-shaven as Cheryl had described him. He was also rather jolly. He welcomed them into his room, offered them chairs and sent for coffee, which arrived on a trolley, wheeled by a tired-looking woman. He had no objection to the interview being taped. He confirmed that the paper was owned by a consortium of three Edinburgh businessmen. He gave their names, which his visitors already knew from the Companies Register. His manner remained friendly but the limit of his helpfulness had already been reached. He knew of no Mr McRitchie nor had he ever been approached by a young woman under either name. It was soon evident that he was much more interested in pumping them for the reasons behind their visit. His manner suggested that he was hoping for a front-page story, but Honey suspected that his real motives were more sinister.

After an hour both parties had reached their peak of frustration. As they got up to leave, Mr Hogwood said, 'Please bear in mind that the officers made no statements and that no conclusions are to be drawn from their questions. Any article published containing material extrapolated from those questions will be scrutinised with care and may well become the subject of proceedings.'

Mr Barclay beamed. 'I note what you say,' he said.

The detective constable, a freckled and ginger-haired young man named Nicholson, joined them as they passed through the hall, giving a small headshake to denote that no significant messages had been passed within his view and no individuals answering to Cheryl's description of McRitchie had materialized. Honey had worked with young Nicholson before. She was aware that he was nicknamed Knickers and, what's more, seemed proud of it.

They got back into the Mercedes. 'Well,' Honey said, 'if they didn't know that they were under investigation, they do now. Perhaps it's for the best. Sometimes that kind of knowledge prods people into action when they might have been well advised to keep perfectly still. Like the rabbit that bolts from under your feet,' she added in explanation. She looked at her watch. 'Lunchtime approaches. Does anyone fancy the canteen or shall we call at Lorelli's.'

DC Nicholson seemed uneasy. Lorelli's was not expensive but it was undeniably dearer than the canteen. Honey was puzzling over how to word an offer to subsidise his meal when Sandy said, 'I'll sign your expenses.'

The constable relaxed.

'Take a quick lunch,' Honey told him, 'and then get back there. There's a pub almost opposite. Watch which of the staff takes lunch there and listen to what's said. There seem to be rooms to rent upstairs. Try to take one for the afternoon and watch who comes and goes. I still want to know what became of McRitchie.'

'Yes,' Sandy said thoughtfully. 'So do I.'

They were early enough at Lorelli's so that tables were free. They seated themselves at the back of the room while they considered the menu. Mr Hogwood had never offered them a first name. He had been sitting and observing in silence as the best solicitors do. Now he stirred. 'Mr Barclay came over well.'

'Too damn well,' said Sandy. 'I went into his room convinced that he was going to be a liar but now I'm not so sure.'

'He's a liar,' said Hogwood. 'He had the smell. I'll tell you something. You asked him about Miss Abernethy and her attempt to sell him a story. You played your hand cleverly. You told him a lot about her. But you never said that she was dead and you never called her black. He was so much distracted by the need never to fall into your more obvious trap and use the past tense that he very nearly slipped up, as our politicians always do, over the colour question. He said, "No blessed girl tried to sell us a story about election expenses, I can assure you." He put it over very calmly and convincingly, as do the very best liars in the witness box. But there was just an instant of hesitation during the word "blessed". He was going to say "black", but he remembered in time that you hadn't told him that bit yet. Very quick thinking.'

'No honest man thinks so quickly,' Honey said.

The restaurant was pleasant and half empty. The food was good. Honey would have preferred to take her time, but the officer from Haddington was due. She had to hurry the others to finish their meals. Hogwood in particular was inclined to linger. He had taken several glasses of the house wine with his lunch, perhaps exceeding what his small body mass could readily absorb, and he wanted to expound on other great liars who he had met and circumvented. Honey had to threaten to call a taxi and begin her expenses claim, with a lengthy explanation of the reasons why the taxi had been necessary, before he could be dislodged in order to transport them back to HQ.

Chief Inspector Jowett, from Haddington, was a lean man, slightly stooped. He had thinning, grey hair, a matching moustache, a swarthy complexion, a sense of his own importance and a chip on his shoulder. His uniform was smart. He was not inclined to forgive Honey for keeping him waiting despite her apologies and it was soon clear that he also resented having been called in by an officer of lesser rank. She invited him to sit but he preferred to stand. What, he demanded, was wrong with the telephone, or email, or fax, or, for the matter of that, radio? He had a squeaky voice that might have been specifically designed to irritate her.

'I am under orders,' Honey said grimly, 'to keep this particular matter totally confidential.'

'Even from your fellow officers? I never heard such rubbish.'

Honey kept her head and her temper. 'All the same, sir, I must request your assurance that you will treat this as confidential and direct any of your officers who you must instruct in the matter to do the same.'

'None of my men would talk out of school.'

His jaw was set. Honey could see that, while she might force him to offer lip service, he would never take his own promise seriously. Well, why have a dog and do your own barking? The short-tempered and over-bearing Detective Superintendent Black-house did have his strengths and she might as well make use of them. She picked up the internal phone and keyed his number. Im-mediately, the voice snapped 'Yes?'

'Detective Inspector Laird here, sir. I have Chief Inspector Jowett of Haddington with me. He is reluctant to give me any assur-ances about confidentiality.'

'Bring him to me.' Such was his tone that Honey was tempted to enquire, All of him or just his head? She managed to resist the temptation. Mr Blackhouse was not noted for his sense of humour.

Honey escorted the chief inspector to the superintendent's door and left them to sort it out between themselves. She returned to her own desk. Chief Inspector Jowett return-ed there about thirty minutes later. He had lost some colour and he looked ten years older. 'It seems that I am to take my briefing from you,' he said stiffly.

The opportunity to bully a higher-ranking officer was tempting but she decided to treat him kindly. Anyone who had suffered a mauling from Mr Blackhouse, and their name was legion, would be in need of consideration. Again she offered him a chair and this time he took it, lowering himself into it gently as if suspecting a trap.

Honey painted a picture of Dougal Walsh. 'He is dangerous,' she said. 'He will be armed. And he's quick with a knife. We want him for two killings. But we want him alive. If recognized, do not under any circumstances alert him. Arrest him if you can do so safely and – this is important – inconspicuously. If not, or if you can track him to his lair, this office is to be advised and we will do it by the book. That is very much to be preferred. You understand?'

'I understand.'

'You may have difficulty in getting your men to watch for him without risking word getting around. If word gets back to him that the police are taking a special interest in him, that could spell disaster. However, you were prepared to speak for the discretion of your men, so perhaps we can trust you to walk that particular tightrope?'

The chief inspector seemed happy to make his escape.

Eighteen

Crime takes notice of the days of the week only so far as opportunities may come or go. Detectives in criminal investigation departments may therefore work much more flexible hours and days than officers on more routine duties. The Lairds, however, having set several enquiries in motion, had little to do but wait.

The line of enquiry that Honey had considered most hopeful turned out to be, for the moment, a dead end. Planning officials, asked whether they had been consulted about planning approval for an oil refinery, revealed a variety of reactions – amusement from those whose territories were already fully developed, interest from those whose areas might benefit from such a development and blank denial from the rest. It was a fairly safe assumption that one of the latter group was dissembling, but that would not be unusual. Planning consents dealing with major industrial developments were as good as huge sums of money in the bank, so the applications were always considered to be slightly more confidential than the sex lives of the councillors, and considerably more important.

Signs of spring were showing in the garden, but the weather gods seemed to have read a different book. The only relief from wind-driven rain was when it turned to short-lived snow. They stayed at home over the weekend. Honey nursed Minka while typing one-handed on her laptop, drafting notes on possible lines of enquiry. Sandy spent much time dozing in his favourite chair, sometimes somnolently taking over nursing duty; but Honey was fairly sure that he too was sifting through the facts and fancies.

On the Sunday evening, while they were watching a totally uninteresting drama on the television, the phone rang. Honey lifted the receiver. The call had been placed from a public telephone. She and Sandy were sitting very close together in the big armchair, so he could hear every word. 'Mrs Laird?' said a voice. It was clearly articulated with only a trace of the Scottish central belt in it, but the voice had a nasal, metallic twang. 'Mrs Laird, this is a very friendly warning. Your present enquiries are likely to be very bad for your health. You must, you really must, let up on your enquiries. If you just drop them you'll attract all the wrong sort of attention. Here's what you must report—'

Honey was about to break in and ask which enquiries. To know whether the voice was referring to Haddington or to the site for the refinery or to the murder of Jem Tanar or any of the other lines of enquiry might have been enlightening. But at that moment Sandy took the phone out of her hand and broke the connection. 'Never reply to that sort of message,' he said. 'Any answer is an acknowledgement, but if they can't make the threat they won't act on it.'

'Next time,' Honey said, 'I'll decide when to hang up.'

'All right. Just so long as you remember my words of wisdom.'

Honey only had to turn her head to be in a position to give him a kiss on the side of the nose. 'I love you when you're masterful, but please confine it to the bedroom. You could at least have listened to what threat or inducement was being offered.'

'It would have been the same old vague, ominous threats of unspecific but terrible consequences. Settle down and watch the play.'

'You watch it,' Honey said, 'if you're mindless enough.'

Twenty minutes later, the phone rang again. Honey put out her hand and withdrew it again. After eight rings the answering machine kicked in. They had never put a personalized message on to it, so it was the standard recording that invited the caller to speak after the tone. Then the call-box noises, followed by the same voice, or one very similar, came over the speaker. The voice was still dispassionate, even slightly amused. 'Don't hang up again,' it said. 'Remember, your baby could have been inside.'

Honey exchanged a puzzled look with her husband. The explanation arrived on the heels of the words. There was a muffled sound from the front of the house and orange light filtered through the curtains. A motorbike pulled noisily away. The light grew and alarmed voices penetrated from the street. Sandy said, 'Fire!' and dashed for the door. Honey followed her instincts and stayed with her baby but she grabbed up the phone. The voice was still talking on it. She found her mobile and keyed the emergency services.

Once the fire service was alerted she had time to swallow the lump in her throat and sift her struggling thoughts. Sandy was the next priority. The curtains were negligible protection, but they gave her a small and precious amount of reassurance. She peeped between them. On the brick-paved parking area that had replaced most of the insignificant front garden, the Range Rover was ablaze. She could feel the heat even through the new double glazing. Sandy seemed to have vanished. Heart in mouth, she decided that he could not possibly have been consumed already. Then she realized that Sandy's car, which had been parked beside the Range Rover, had also vanished. Her mind zigzagged. Had he set off in pursuit of the perpetrators? Then, with a surge of relief, she recognized his car, untidily parked across somebody's driveway on the other side of the street.

The first fire engine arrived and began to coat everything with foam. Traffic was backing up in all directions. Flames were replaced by smoke and smells. Drivers began to U-turn, making much use of horns.

She had alerted the police. They seemed to be taking their time. Then she saw that two police Traffic cars had already arrived and Sandy was talking to the officers.

She waited, disconsolate and alone. The world had gone slightly out of focus. The room, usually so comforting, looked strange. It was as if each decision, lovingly made to assemble the environment they craved, had been minutely wrong. She spent her days sorting out the tangles and deciding the rights and wrongs and the culpability of crimes directed against others, but when she herself was the victim there was a shift in perspective. The rules had been broken. Sandy's had been, she conceded mentally, the sensible action – to save the one car that was not burning. All the same, she felt indignant that the car destroyed was hers, much the more expensive and just when she had got everything the way she wanted it. Some of her favourite CDs were stacked in the multi-changer. Her Barbour and green wellingtons had just been returned by hand of the Northern motorcyclist who was acting as courier, and with the manufacturer Hunter in liquidation the boots might be difficult to replace.

As always in times of stress, once the first panic was over her tidy mind began to arrange the future into a sensible pattern. She phoned her father. Having a rich father might sometimes be a drag but more often it could afford a huge relief. Happily, her father was at home. He came on the line just as Sandy, looking both drawn and soot-stained, entered the room. She studied him carefully but he had not lost any skin or hair.

'Dad,' she said, speaking as much to Sandy as to her father, 'we've been threatened and to back it up somebody just fired the Range Rover. We don't know what might follow, so Sandy and I will probably go to a hotel. Minka would be safer with you, with gardeners and gamekeepers all over the place. Could you send somebody through to collect her and June and all her chattels?' She raised her eyebrows at Sandy but he was already nodding.

'Yes, of course,' said her father.

'And my wellies were in the back. There's an old pair in the downstairs cloakroom. Would you have somebody add them to the load? Next, the Range Rover's a write-off. If you're still of the same mind...?'

'No problem,' said her father. 'I can use one of the other cars until I can put my hand on the four-by-four that I really want. I'll send the Range Rover through at the same time. That way the driver can come back with the rest of the menagerie.'

'I'll pass on the insurance money when it comes.'

When they disconnected, Sandy said, 'How long have we got?'

'Allowing him a little time to get organized, an hour, maybe more.'

'You'd better break it to June as soon as she comes in. I'll try to arrange for a couple of armed officers to stay here, just in case.'

'Fine. Then book us into a hotel.' She drew a deep breath. 'Then come and tell me what you want to bring with you, so that I know what to pack. And bring the tape out of the answering machine. Somebody may be able to tell something from it.'

'Slow down,' Sandy said. 'You're doing very well but you're going hyperactive again. I suggest that you gather your wits and phone in a short report.'

'The story of my life,' Honey said gloomily. 'Is the front of the house much marked?'

'Nothing that won't scrub off,' said Sandy. 'The insurance will cover it.'

'I take it that nobody was injured?'

'I think Humphrey Blake next door messed his pants. He can claim off our insurance if he doesn't mind explaining how it happened.'

A room was reserved for them at a comfortable but not extravagant hotel, although it was after midnight before they were able to retire to it.

June had arrived at the house in a state of shock after seeing and smelling the aftermath of the fire, but once reassured as to the safety of Minka, and then of her employers, she took the news that she was to return to Perthshire without complaint. It would mean working under her mother's jaundiced eye, but on the other hand she would once again have almost a monopoly of both Minka and Pippa. No doubt the presence on the estate of several keepers, as many gardeners and two handyman/chauffeurs (not all of them ancient and married) was an added inducement.

Mr Potterton-Phipps arrived after little more than the hour, driving the promised Range Rover but accompanying a Volvo estate. By that time the burned Range Rover had been removed to the police garage for study and only the scorched brick paving and a smell of burnt rubber and plastic remained as a sad reminder of what had been. A mountain of baby clothes and equipment took up much of the Volvo's huge carrying capacity. Pippa's bed filled one of the rear passenger's seats. Mr Potterton-Phipps, travelling beside his chauffeur, refused to have her at his feet so she occupied her bed for the trip. June took Minka, in her travelling cot, on her knees. As the car drove off, Honey could see Pippa's anxious eyes reflecting the headlamps of a passing taxi and she sent the dog telepathic messages of reassurance, that this was not a permanent parting or removal.

Sandy's attention was given over to answering questions from Headquarters, provoked by Honey's first report. Whoever had threatened them and fired the Range Rover might be very interested in any such discussions so he made his answers very guarded, referring their colleagues to Mr Blackhouse if they wanted more details. This, of course, entailed a report in person to Mr Black-house, who lived halfway across the city. It was left to Honey, after the departure of her father and the rest of her family, to gather up everything that they would or might need in exile and to prepare for the two armed officers who were to occupy the house in their absence. She packed clothes. When the supply of suitcases ran out, cardboard cartons were called into use. She familiarized herself with the new Range Rover. This appeared to be even more luxurious than its predecessor and the colour, she thought, was quite acceptable though it was difficult to judge under the artificial lights. She emptied the ashtray and loaded luggage, files and computers, all this while reassuring solicitous neighbours that she and Sandy were unharmed and were not making a permanent evacuation.

Back indoors there wasn't time for fear or regret. It remained to get the house ready for strangers. Guns were already in the gun-safe, which itself was in a lockable cupboard behind a solid oak door. It was joined by all the wines and spirits in the house. Grateful as she was for the provision of the armed officers, she was not so grateful as to give them free access to the carefully chosen and expensively purchased drink. The beer, they could have and welcome.

The two officers turned up before she was finished, in plain clothes and a car which, she was pleased to note, was just the kind that she might have hired in a hurry. They comprised a heavily built constable and a slim and rather effeminate sergeant who was undoubtedly male and turned out later to be proficient in every one of the martial arts. They appreciated the arrangements that had been made for them, but Honey made it clear that if there were any damages to *Chief* Inspector Laird's house, their guns would not save them.

She then took them exhaustively through all the idiosyncrasies of the house: the timer on the boiler and who to call if it leaked again; how to work the microwave and the dishwasher; how to programme the DVD recorder; the fact that two channels on the main TV were swapped over on the remote control and all the other little quirks that occur in the best regulated houses. The penultimate lecture was on the food in the two freezers; which they might eat and which were to be considered sacrosanct. In the event of incoming phone calls, every effort was to be made to check the identity of the caller and only those with impeccable identities were to be given her or Sandy's mobile number.

Sandy returned at last. Later, he excused

himself for his tardiness by explaining that he had had to await the return of Mr and Mrs Blackhouse from the theatre and that, after some prompting from Mrs Blackhouse, he had been invited inside for coffee. He described Mrs Blackhouse as a charmer, which Honey already knew. He was about to start the briefing of the two visitors all over again until Honey told him, through gritted teeth, that she had *said* all that and she was now moving out with every intention of going to bed in the hotel. And, she added, she was not going to bed in a strange hotel with the door unlocked. Sandy wound up his peroration and they got on the road.

Lothian and Borders encompasses a lot of territory, so Sandy was quite accustomed to sleeping away from home, but Honey still found going to bed, and even more so getting up, strangely unencumbered with no dog to walk and no chores to do, as rather foreign. As a consequence, they arrived at HQ in unusually good time in the morning. Honey, seeing her new car in daylight for the first time, decided that her father was being unduly picky – or, at least, that the colour would stop making her feel bilious after a month or two.

Sandy had an office to himself, which he had embellished with a few carefully chosen watercolours. For the sake of confidentiality, they had agreed to share this room and his desk for as long as they were working in harness. Honey visited her own desk to collect whatever had come in over the weekend and then settled down while Sandy bustled away to make a fuller report of the current status quo and to deposit the answering machine tape with Forensics in the hope that somebody could extract some extra information about people or places. Working on the wrong side of the desk gave her inadequate knee-room but she could use her laptop where the designer had intended – on her lap.

Police motorcyclists must have been buzzing about all night, or else rendezvous had been arranged between Traffic cars of different forces, because a lot of material had accumulated. Much of it, however, was negative. The post mortem examination on the dead girl, for instance, had been completed. The report ran to many pages without revealing more than that she had died of a single stab wound, that the wound appeared to have been inflicted by the knife that had been left in the body and that she had suffered from a facial blemish – but had otherwise been in perfect health. Her skin was otherwise unmarked, by which was meant that there were no signs of ligatures or violence. As already reported, she had died during the act of sex or very soon afterwards, prior to which she had not been a virgin but nor had she been unduly promiscuous. Bodily fluids, presumably those of her killer, had been recovered from the body and would provide DNA evidence.

The other autopsy, that of Jem Tanar, had also concluded. He had suffered three stab wounds; any one of which might have been fatal and all of which might well have been inflicted by the same knife as was believed to have killed the girl, but that could not be confirmed. He had been a user of hard drugs although at the time of his death he had been almost clean. Apart from lingering traces of a sexually transmitted disease, the report said little else that could not have been said of a thousand others.

The fee-paying school attended by Cheryl Abernethy had been traced. Honey's spirits rose, only to fall again. The school was on the outskirts of Glasgow, close to a busy commuter railway station, so that only the vaguest approximation of the family's location could be deduced. The school records had been transferred to computer by an incompetent and only partially literate typist and recovering them was proving to be laborious and sometimes a matter of guesswork. No Abernethy family had so far been

217

found on either side of the Firth of Forth.

Seven MPs (European, Westminster or Scottish) had constituencies that could be considered to accord with the known facts. It was evident that enquiries had been made with less than the required tact, because two of the six gentlemen, but not the one presumed lady, had made firm but polite enquiries as to why their election expenses were being subjected to scrutiny. Each was expecting a written reply. Honey made a face at the wall. This could become nasty. It did indeed become nastier later in the morning when one of them, the supposedly Honourable Geoffrey Manquers MSP, came in personally to reinforce his objection to the matter of his election expenses being raised again. He was a distinguished-looking man in his fifties with hair that was silver rather than white or grey. He had an elevated opinion of himself. Honey passed him over to Mr Blackhouse and returned to Sandy's room while wondering whether Mr Manquers was the parliamentarian that they were seeking. He had certainly looked at her figure with eyes that seemed to see through her clothes, which did rather suggest the libertine described by Cheryl Abernethy.

A note from PC Knickers reported that he had listened to the chatting of the newspaper staff in the pub, but the only references to what must have been an unusual regime had been of puzzlement. It seemed that nobody below the levels of the managing editor and his deputy knew what was going on. Nobody answering the description of McRitchie had emerged from the building, nor had the name been mentioned in his hearing. In all likelihood, Honey thought, McRitchie had been sent on holiday, or on a course, and his colleagues had been told that he was ill. Alternatively, he might have been disposed of and his colleagues told that he had gone to another job. There was no way to find out without setting alarm bells ringing.

Sandy returned, bearing two coffees. Honey suddenly felt thirsty and in need of sugar for her mental energy. While she satisfied both needs, she briefed Sandy on the weekend's traffic. 'That's an awful lot of words for bugger all,' Sandy said. He had brought a transcript. 'Look at this,' he said. 'They're still trying to identify the accent and the voice-print, but the message is interesting.'

Honey began reading.

Don't hang up. Remember your baby could have been inside. It's your choice, both of you. A dead baby or twenty grand in the bank, plus your insurance of course. Wherever you go we can find you.

All you have to do is to report that the black tart's death was down to her pimp, Doug Briar, and nothing to do with anything else. If you need witnesses to back up any story, put a vase of flowers in the window over your front door and you'll be phoned. But don't try any tricks or we'll know. You won't be the first copper on the payroll. And you wouldn't be the first to suffer bereavement for not playing ball.

'I'm sending the original tape through to Mr Halliday by the next courier,' Sandy said. 'Strathclyde may be able to home in on that voice or get some clue from the background street noises. I don't think we need let the threat bother us too much. With all your father's staff warned to watch out for strangers, and most of them having dandled you on their hairy knees, I wouldn't give much for a Glasgow thug's chance of getting at Minka and none whatever for his chance of getting away again.'

Honey was not sure that that was quite enough, but she was reassured when her father phoned her mobile early in the afternoon. 'I've handed over the responsibility to the best security firm I know and the only one I'm prepared to trust my granddaughter's safety to,' Mr Potterton-Phipps said cheerfully. 'My staff and the hired guards now know each other individually, so if anybody sneaks in he's the Invisible Man.'

'Thank you, Dad,' Honey said. It occurred to her that this conversation was in breach of the agreement to avoid passing sensitive information over a line that could be tapped. On the other hand, when it came to her child's safety, perhaps it was best that the opposition knew what it was up against. 'I'm sorry if I'm putting you to a lot of expense.'

'Think nothing of it. Nothing's too good for my youngest grandchild and this is injecting a little excitement into a life that was, frankly, beginning to bore me.'

Honey could not imagine how a bustling life that alternated between top-level business meetings and top-of-the-range shooting and fishing engagements could possibly be boring, but she said, 'That's all right then,' in a weak voice.

'About your other questions—'

'Not on the phone, please, Dad. I'll call you from a secure phone this evening.'

'I was only going to report a lack of progress,' her father said plaintively. 'I'm having to go all round the houses to find what you want. Minka's here. Would you like to speak to her?'

Custom required that she make cooing noises down the phone but Sandy was out of the room and the desk phone was ringing. A motorcyclist was trying to hand her a package of papers and Mr Blackhouse's bulky form was looming in the doorway. 'Give her my love,' Honey said, 'and tell her that I'll call her when I have time.' She could feel her father's disapproval filtering down the phone but there was a limit to the number of simultaneous conversations that she could sustain.

Nineteen

With Minka safely tucked away and guarded, it seemed unlikely that direct physical action would be attempted against her parents. The criminal fraternity learned many decades ago that knocking off the detectives in charge of a case only intensified the pursuit and increased the penalties – if the assailant managed to survive long enough to make a court appearance. By coincidence, killers of police officers have been known to suffer unfortunate accidents. The Lairds would, however, have preferred to change hotels regularly in order to avoid any sort of harassment. Honey stopped off on the way to the office next morning to make a booking for the following day and she watched her rear mirror with such care that she nearly ran into the back of a bus.

As a result, she was slightly after her usual time when she arrived. Sandy was out of the room, engaged in his usual morning conference with Mr Blackhouse. Waiting patiently beside the vacant desk was a plainclothes constable – from Haddington, he announced. With a flutter of anticipation, Honey seated herself on her side of Sandy's desk. 'Go on,' she said.

'Madam. Chief Inspector Jowett's compliments, and we've spotted your man.'

Honey felt a big grin escaping. Then she sobered. 'How?'

The man relaxed. 'I went for a snack in a caff last night and there he was. There was something rang a bell and when I looked against the light I could see the make-up covering the stain. And I heard him speak to the girl at the till. Pure Gorbals.'

'You didn't alert him, I hope?'

The constable smiled. He was young and keen but Honey thought that she could trust him. 'No risk of that, ma'am. I had my own car with me so I went out and waited. When he came out, all wrapped up in leathers, he got on a motorbike. An old Norton it was but it sounded healthy. I followed him from a long way back, out into the country. There was other traffic, so he'd no call to get nervous. In the end, from half a mile off, I saw his lamp stop where I know there's an old cottage, not much more than a shack. Minutes later there was smoke and sparks at the chimney like somebody had made up the fire. I waited, just in case he came out again, but he never did. An old man used to live there, but he died last summer. I asked around, very careful, and this is his grandson. I've written the location by Sat Nav down for you.' He handed over a slip of paper, then drew himself up again. 'Mr Jowett said as how I'd been the one to spot him so I could have the pleasure of giving you the news.'

It seemed that Chief Inspector Jowett had a trace of humanity after all. Honey spared some seconds for thought. 'Thank you. You have made a young inspector very happy. And please thank Mr Jowett for me. Now, get back and go on being careful. We'd like observation kept but very carefully. We'd rather lose him than alarm him. Above all, if he gets suspicious he must not be allowed to pass the news. If any officer thinks he's been sussed, Walsh is to be arrested immediately and kept incommunicado. Got it?'

'Got it, ma'am.'

'Keep it all very low-key and secret but stay in touch with your control room – we'll need you to guide us in.'

'Yes, ma'am.' The tone was one of enthusiasm.

Honey was immediately prey to a not unfamiliar sensation of needing to do half a dozen things, each of which took priority over all the others. She plucked the temporary cellphone out of her shoulder bag, treating it to a sneer as she did so, because she considered it very cheap and nasty compared to her own top-of-the-range model.

After a short argument with a trusted underling, she got Chief Superintendent Halliday on the cellphone. Honey made a very brief report.

'Does Mr Blackhouse know?'

'I'm just about to report to him.'

'Good. Do that. Then call me again and let me speak to him.'

Honey hurried down to the detective superintendent's office. Other officers were awaiting the big man's attention, but she persuaded them to scatter by promising each of them priority on the morrow. When she was finally alone with Mr Blackhouse and Sandy she broke the good news. At the same time she keyed the digit for Strathclyde. 'Mr Halliday wants to speak to you.'

'How the hell did he get on to it so quickly?'

Honey shrugged.

Of the three senior officers, one belonged to Lothian and Borders and one to Northern; yet Mr Halliday, though lacking the authority afforded by a corpse, outranked the others. During the discussion that followed it was noticeable that Mr Blackhouse was showing unusual respect. It was also noticeable that he now faced an even quicker and more forceful organizer than himself. When he finally switched off the cellphone and returned it to her he looked, Honey thought, as if he'd drunk from somebody's cough medicine in error instead of his own vodka and tonic.

'I do not believe in undue haste,' he said. 'I would rather gather our forces, lay our plans and move in at dawn. Mr Halliday fears that the man may take fright and go. He's coming through almost immediately. I said that I couldn't be sure of rustling up enough armed and trained officers for a proper cordon so quickly – and, according to the book, we should have two cordons – so he said that he would bring some of his own men on loan.'

'We've no reason to believe that the man has a firearm,' Sandy said. 'He seems to prefer a knife.'

'That doesn't mean that he won't have one now. But we're to make sure that everyone understands that we want this man alive.' Mr Blackhouse seemed to become aware that Honey was still standing. 'Do sit down, inspector. I'll leave it to you to see how many personnel we have available who're qualified to go armed. In two hours' time, gather them together – incommunicado, to use your own word. Better lay on a coach and hold them in that. Feed them first.' He turned to Sandy. 'You and I can draft a plan of operations. See

227

if you can get your hands on a copy of the ordnance survey plan.'

As she rose to go, Honey noticed that a nudge on the end of the superintendent's out-tray would push a large mug of hot coffee off the edge of his desk and into his lap, but, nobly, she denied herself the pleasure. She had become used to being treated as a female and therefore an inferior gofer.

Although Honey enjoyed testing her skills on game birds and clay pigeons, she was not bloodthirsty by nature. All the same, by mid-afternoon she was distinctly miffed. The fire-arms course that she had passed with flying colours during her time with the Met had also been the occasion when she first met Sandy. The qualification to wear a side arm thus had a sentimental significance for her. She had spent the middle of the day frantically gathering up every qualified officer that she could find, sometimes almost physically having to wrest them away from the leaders of their present teams. She had confiscated their personal mobile phones and impounded their radios pending their release from the coach and their collective weight rested on the rear seat of the Range Rover. She had somehow contrived to arrange for them to be fed without any word leaking beyond the catering staff.

And now, here she was, sitting at the wheel of her own car, armed but left on the sidelines. The two superintendents and Sandy had ridden in the coach and briefed the officers there, but it seemed to have been decided – and Honey suspected that Sandy had had a hand in it – that she was much too valuable to risk in the firing line. She had always resented any attempt to leave her out of the action on grounds of gender, but in her mind this was undoubtedly what was afoot. Yet it had been clear from the final report on the firearms course that she was a better and safer pistol shot than Sandy. If she found that he had spread word to the contrary just to keep her safe it might be gratifying, but he would nevertheless be punished. A counter-rumour, to the effect that during his time in the States his American colleagues had refused to accompany him if he was armed, should do the trick. Americans, themselves the masters of Friendly Fire, can get touchy on the subject. She was wearing a 9mm Smith and Wesson semi-automatic in a holster on her hip and under the jacket of her cashmere suit, but she had been relegated to following the coach in her own car. This was on the insubstantial grounds that separate transport might be required and hers was the car least likely to be recognized by the opposition. She was to act as an emergency backstop, behind the cordon, possibly standing by to convey prisoner and guard back to Edinburgh. She sat and seethed.

Now that the die was cast the personal radios were back in use. The motorcycle officer who had brought the tidings that morning had met them several miles short of Haddington and, bypassing that pleasant small town, had led them in the direction of the Lammermuirs. Almost immediately they had escaped from the hustle and bustle of Edinburgh traffic and its A-roads into the B-roads that wandered through fertile farmland. The coach had been abandoned behind a rural pub, by arrangement with a landlord who probably expected boom business when the operation was over.

The long file of armed officers was led by the motorcycle policeman, on foot for once. It vanished over a fold in the ground and through some trees. Honey was summoned by radio to bring her car up a short stretch of farm access road and then take to a track between two hillocks of tumbledown boulders where farming, forestry and building were all quite impossible and only rabbits thrived.

She settled down to wait in a flattened space used as a machinery dump, between a multi-gang plough and a rusty harrow, while the daylight turned pink and the sun sagged lower in the sky, painting the layers of cloud in discordant colours.

She had no view of the cottage where Dougal Walsh was holed up, but by the occasional radio traffic she could follow the laying of the trap as the cordon was pulled around the cottage. From her earlier study of the map, she could tell that they had approached the cottage from the rear. She heard her husband's voice directing two men to a position where they could close off any frontal arrival or departure.

Early rain had died away leaving puddles to reflect the dying sun, but the day remained dank and cold. She had half-turned the Range Rover so that she could see the farmhouse and its attendant barns. The farmer parked his tractor in one of the barns and went indoors. A fox came through the boulders, sniffing for young rabbits. Crows were streaming and tumbling steadily to roost. It was a peaceful scene, with the land laid out in a patchwork of different greens and browns. Relegated to the position of a waiting chauffeur, Honey soon found her eyes heavy. She began to doze. She could picture Minka on her grandfather's estate, being proudly exhibited by June. The sound of the crows became the voices of the admiring throng.

She snapped awake as the voices on the radio became more urgent. A sound reached her but not via the radio. It could have been a distant hammer blow or the popping of a paper bag. It sounded too insignificant to have been a shot but, Honey reminded herself, any but the largest handguns make no more than a feeble-sounding pop when fired out of doors. That it had been a gunshot was confirmed immediately by a roar over the radio, in what was undoubtedly the voice of Detective Superintendent Blackhouse, reminding all and sundry that they wanted the man alive. Whether the shot had been fired by Dougal Walsh or by one of the cordon remained unclear. What did seem clear was that any shot had failed to find a mark.

Another sound was rising above the hiss and crackle of the radio and the cawing of crows on their way to roost. Surely Dougal Walsh did not have a microlight aircraft available? If so, they had probably lost him. Then she remembered the old Norton and the sound resolved itself into a powerful but old-fashioned, low-revving motorbike engine. It took her several seconds to judge from the growing volume that it was coming in her general direction. It could have been heading past her on another track, but she thought not. She hesitated before remembering that she had the only vehicle on the scene. She started the Range Rover's engine and engaged gear, but before she could pull forward and block what there was of a pathway between the rocks, the motorbike reared up into the gap, bounced spectacularly, executed a majestic wobble, recovered balance and roared across the flattened ground to her front. It seemed that Dougal Walsh had leaped into the saddle without waiting to dress for motorcycling on a damp day. His helmet dangled from the handlebars and he was in shirtsleeves.

Twenty

It was instinctive to pursue. A wild animal is programmed to follow when another runs away. Honey threw the Range Rover forward and dragged it round. The permanent four-wheel drive gave the powerful vehicle a formidable acceleration. A spur of rock lunged at her and without the power steering she could never have swerved in time. Then the Norton was a dark blob fleeing down the farm road in front of her. She put her foot down and prayed that this Range Rover handled identically at speed to the one that had burned.

On the straight, she could spare a small fragment of her attention for reporting in. Luckily the car had a hands-free system. The radio was already live, but to make sure she keyed the two digits for Mr Blackhouse's phone into her own mobile. 'I'm in pursuit,' she said loudly. 'Heading towards Haddington.'

There was immediate babble, which resolved itself into Mr Blackhouse's voice telling her to hold the man in view, keep reporting, but under no circumstances whatever was she to become involved. This was competing with Sandy's voice saying much the same thing.

The farm road was rough and potholed. She could see that the rider in front of her could choose an almost straight path avoiding the potholes. He was standing on his footrests, allowing the bike to bounce between his thighs. Lacking any such tactic for cushioning the bumps, she could only try to pick the nearest approximation to a flat surface that she could find and try to leave the worst of the potholes to one side or between the wheels. The farm road remained more or less straight. She managed to gabble a few more words of acknowledgement and report. Over the radio she heard requests for local cars to be alerted and moved ahead to intercept at some unspeciified point.

The Range Rover had been built with just such abuse in mind and was generally recognized as the best all terrain vehicle in general use, but she still hated to think what she was doing to the suspension. Her insides were being bounced and jostled. The tarmac would come as a blessed relief. But evidently her quarry knew the layout. Just before they returned to a solid road, he turned off on to a track that undulated along behind a ragged strip of conifers.

She made the same turn and managed another fragment of report while she considered tactics. She had switched on the Sat Nav but with the car bouncing and juddering she could obtain only the vaguest impression of the map. Her best hope was that he would arrive at a closed gate. The gap between them was such that she would be able to reach him before he could get through and close the gate against her. And what then? She had her handgun but nobody knew how he might be armed and he was very much wanted alive. He knew the lie of the land. If he had spent much time here he would have ridden the paths and tracks many times. He knew that she was following. From time to time he twisted to look back and the machine wobbled dangerously. His mind would be turning over just the same sort of calculation. There would be places where two wheels could go but four could not.

The track curled around a great heap of boulders and then forked. The motorcycle turned away uphill, away from the town. The hardwood trees of the farmland were replaced by coniferous planting, closing in on both sides. Much of the surface was worn down while the roots of the conifers, being shallow, made ridges across the track. It was traditional washboard surface. It came back to her that the best ride over such a surface came when the speed was either very high or very low. She accelerated. The ride improved. Despite the bouncing and the narrowness of the track, she managed to refocus her eyes for moments at a time and read the coordinates off the Sat Nav. She relayed them through the radio. Her colleagues should now be dashing round by tarmac, but it would be a long hike on foot to the coach and even then it was doubtful whether the coach could approach near to where she was being led. They might be using a commandeered tractor and trailer, to turn him back, or perhaps the local panda cars were massing on his route. But the whole spread of the Lammermuirs was ahead, with fences, bogs, forestry and every kind of obstacle, but very few roads.

The washboard surface seemed smoother as she picked up more speed. Trees were rushing past, in places so close that she felt the urge to pull her elbows in; but only the greenery reached far enough to brush the sides of the car. The exposed roots were slippery. She was gaining ground. She pushed forward, closing on his rear wheel. He looked round. She could see the stain on his face. She was just considering a ramming tactic when he swerved suddenly on to a grassy slope. He bounced, slithered and vanished uphill among pine trees. The receding scene was increasingly dark, so she knew that the pinewood closed in. This was the one place where a motorcycle could probably go, but the trees would be too close together for a Range Rover.

She held the car steady while she called in a quick report and position fix, then she kept her foot down, hammering up the track over the roots. She felt a little guilty. She had been brought up where every girl learned to ride as soon as she could straddle a Shetland pony and she had never got out of the habit of thinking of her car as a living being, to be exercised, perhaps stretched but never knowingly injured. However, her only chance now was to put on all possible speed and try to make her way in the same general direction as that taken by the Norton, hoping for a glimpse, a distant engine-note, a tyreprint or perhaps even a chance dog-walker who had seen or heard the Norton. The small map of the Sat Nav was too limited to be of much help. Her recollection of a brief glimpse of the Ordnance Survey map some hours earlier suggested that he could only go onward. There was no other track leading back down towards the town, of that she was sure. Of course, he could circle somewhere among the trees and return to the track behind her, but she thought not. He would not know what pursuit was following on.

There was brighter sky in front of her. The track that she was on reached a crest and emerged from the woods. Mingled grass and heather stretched ahead, rising towards the skyline and dotted with sheep. The track forked. Walsh could not have crossed in front of her yet, so she turned left and recovered speed. Of course, he might have come to a dead end or been turned by the sight of her fellow officers. He could be racing back to meet her. She kept up her speed but felt the pistol on her belt and loosened it in the holster. It was of small calibre and just what use it might be in the event of a collision she could not have said, but she was in a mood to grasp at straws.

More conifers rose ahead, this time a plantation, fenced against deer. The track arrived at a T-junction. She stopped, switched off and got out. Somewhere in the distance she could hear the stammer of the motorbike. She held her breath and turned her head. The sound was coming from in front of her and to the left. The leftward arm of the junction seemed to be curving in the right direction. She reported quickly. An unidentified voice said, 'We've got his girl-friend in custody.'

Then she heard Sandy's voice. 'He doesn't

have a girlfriend. He uses prostitutes. Show her to the locals. Or try somebody from Vice Squad.'

Honey was already on the move again.

She was meeting a new hazard. The track had been shaped over many years by tractors and trailers. The deep ruts made by their wheels had left a central hump of grass and heather and occasional boulders. She thrust on, trying to keep two wheels on the hump and two on what little rough verge she could find. She ignored so far as she could the scraping and swishing and occasional clatter from beneath.

The track continued to curve in the right direction but it was deteriorating. There were stout trees ahead, close to each side of the track. She had to settle the car down over the central hump. Almost immediately, a boulder caught the underside of the car. There was a heavy crunch and she stopped dead, almost hitting her nose on the windscreen. Thankfully, the airbags did not deploy. The engine was still running but she killed it. The sump might have lost its oil but perhaps she could still save something from the wreckage. In the sudden stillness her mind ran free. She trod down a mad thought that she should draw her pistol and put the vehicle out of its pain.

She used her personal radio again, to

report the disaster and give the co-ordinates of her precise position. She had hardly finished when she became aware of an intrusive noise. She could still hear the Norton. And it was getting louder. The little map on the small screen could hardly be expected to show every small farm track but the lie of the land suggested that the track had been about to come to an end. Or else Dougal Walsh had arrived at a police cordon or some insurmountable obstruction. Either way, he had turned back.

She quitted the car. However much damage she had already inflicted on the Range Rover in the course of duty, she did not intend to invite bullet holes. What's more, she did not know what calibre of pistol Dougal Walsh was carrying. Some pistol bullets, she knew, would go through a car door but only something like a magnum had much chance of going though a pine tree. She stepped close to the stoutest tree nearby and drew her own inadequate weapon, cocked it and left the safety catch off.

Walsh had rounded a bend and was in sight, no more than eighty yards away. The light was going and he looked huge in the dusk. She heard the engine note hesitate as he saw the Range Rover in his path. In the moment of comparative quiet, she stepped out and raised her voice. 'Armed police,' she

cried. 'Stop and throw down your weapon.'
The cry came back as an echo, but she never
knew from where.

The Norton came on, accelerating.

Honey took a two-handed grip, clasping
her right wrist in her left hand. She had
claimed that particular weapon because she
had fired it often before at the range. She
could hardly make out the sights in the poor
light but that shouldn't matter – a pistol is
designed to shoot where its handler is looking. She fired at his front tyre. She heard the
bullet strike metal. Later, her bullet was
found in one of the front forks.

Walsh braked, the motorcycle skidding to a
halt a stone's throw away. His legs went out
to balance the machine. The Norton's head-
lamp came on. It was the sudden blaze that
told them how close darkness was.

Everything went slow. She was dazzled.
Her Smith and Wesson had fallen to her side
and weighed a ton. Walsh raised his own
pistol, copying, as he thought, her two-handed grip. There was nothing left but to die
bravely. She never heard the shot but felt a
blow on the left shoulder such as she might
have got from a carpenter's hammer. There
was pain but it was within the bounds of
tolerance. Her left hand had lost its grip. She
expected his second and fatal shot at any
instant. She took a step to the side, heaved

her pistol up and fired, single-handed.

In slow motion, it seemed, the Norton fell on its side, pinning his leg beneath, but he still held the pistol. She had to turn her back on him in order to reach in through the window and switch on the Range Rover's headlights.

The radio was still open. 'We're both dead,' she said hoarsely. 'Come quickly. Get paramedics.' She had intended to say that they were both shot but she couldn't make the effort to correct her words.

Her shoulder was beginning to hurt like hell but she was damned if she was going to pass out and leave him armed. She walked unsteadily towards him.

There was a very long pause. Walsh was lying on his side. The hot exhaust was burning its way through his jeans and probably through his leg. She tried not to recognize the smell. His pistol was pointing at the ground and his stained face to the sky. He was making a sound that she could only think of as a prolonged moan. And then she saw.

His pistol was of a larger calibre than hers but it was similarly semi-automatic. He had taken a grip, as an amateur often will, by wrapping his left hand around his right hand, thumb on top. No semi-automatic pistol has enough space for two thicknesses of hand between the action body and the slide as it recoils to reload after a shot. His pistol was jammed on his right hand and left thumb.

Honey stepped forward. Walsh was hit. Something was leaking through his shirt. He wrenched his hand free, leaving a lot of skin behind, but he was too late. He looked at her with an expression compounded by a fear of her weapon and a fear of her femininity. Honey said, 'This is for the black girl.' Any movement was agony but she was not going to leave him armed. She swatted him with her pistol, just above the ear. Her pistol was too light to do much damage. He was never out but he was hurt. He was still trying to raise the pistol so she hit him again. 'That's for making holes in my best cashmere,' she said thickly. She kicked his pistol away.

The pain was unbearable. She could feel herself going. The Norton was too hard and hot to fall on. Leaves and pine needles would be better but the man would be better still. The rescue party arrived minutes later and found her sprawled across him, their blood mingling.

Twenty-One

Sandy, thanks to his ability at map reading, was the first arrival, leading a small posse. Mr Blackhouse, by virtue of his bulk, arrived last and dangerously out of breath. Sandy took charge. After one agonized study of his wife he relinquished the care of the wounded to those with first-aid experience and turned his own attention to giving the prisoner the statutory warning whether he could hear it or not, calling up support vehicles to the nearest roadway, organizing stretcher parties and even summoning a farmer with his tractor to pull the Range Rover free and clear.

Of all this Honey, who had lost a great deal of blood and was losing more, remained totally unaware.

It was the end of a long day for Sandy before a preliminary report had been made to the uppermost echelons, the handguns were cleaned and returned to store and the personnel were chivvied out of the pub, thanked and returned whence they came. A careful examination had determined that the

Range Rover would need a new exhaust, but there was no oil leakage and the vehicle was driveable. Even the Norton had been brought to the police garage.

Sandy had managed to keep track of Honey's progress by means of occasional hasty phone calls. She and the prisoner had both been taken to the New Royal Infirmary at Little France. This also happened to be the nearest hospital with staff experienced in treating bullet wounds. It was late in the evening before Sandy was free to visit the hospital and by then Honey was in surgery. The bullet, he was told, had clipped her shoulder, damaging the joint. It had been clear of the major blood vessel or she might easily have bled to death. As it was, she had lost a great deal of blood and this had to be replaced by transfusion before she was strong enough to face surgery. Dougal Walsh, being more seriously injured, had already been on the table for some time in another theatre, but arrangements had been made for a guard to be posted over him when he was returned to a ward, for purposes of both confinement and protection. At the moment of impact of Honey's bullet he had been transformed from the servant of his masters to a very definite threat.

There seemed to be nothing useful for Sandy to do. He had come provided with flowers, which he left along with a message that he thoughtfully gave to several different nurses, human memory being what it so often was. He then retired to his hotel and to bed.

In the morning, anxiety woke Sandy early. A call to the hospital assured him that his wife was out of the anaesthetic, out of immediate danger and sleeping naturally. He drove to police HQ but Detective Superintendent Blackhouse, who had had almost as hard a day, had not hurried to come in. There were messages, of a generally congratulatory nature, from Mr Halliday and Mr Largs. He felt quite unable to settle to any routine, and when the hospital, in response to his eleventh phone call, told him that Honey was now awake and that he could visit, he was in his car and on the move within seconds.

Honey was in a high dependency room just off an orthopaedic ward. A very young but apparently competent doctor gave Sandy a briefing on his wife's condition before allowing him to enter. His own flowers were prominently displayed, as were offerings from Mr Largs and Mr Halliday. Mr Blackhouse, it seemed, had not troubled himself. Honey, with her shoulder and left arm strapped, splinted and supported, was propped up but dozing in the aftermath of the

247

anaesthetic. She roused almost immediately and gave him her special smile.

Sandy hesitated between several different openings. 'Does it hurt much?' he asked.

She considered the question seriously. 'I don't feel it,' she said at last. 'I'm probably stoned on morphine and it'll hurt like hell when that wears off. Tell me something. I seem to remember firing at him. Did I hit him or am I dreaming? The doctors won't tell me a damn thing except that a man was brought in at the same time. They waffle on about medical confidentiality.'

It was Sandy's turn for thought. He wanted to hug her but that was out of the question. He stooped for a kiss. How would Honey feel about having shot a man in anger? Would she have nightmares? He gave a mental shrug. She would find out some time and it was part of his philosophy that truth was best, usually. 'You nailed him,' he said. 'I don't know all the details but one lung had collapsed. His spine was hit. They don't know yet whether he'll walk again. They spent most of the night putting him back together. He's in Intensive Care.'

Even a hospital bed, a drip and several pounds of dressings and splints could not dampen Honey's humour for long. 'And he nearly missed me? Honour is satisfied. All those hours on the range weren't wasted.'

'Certainly not. They probably saved your life. He's in Intensive Care and you're only in High Dependency, which must tell us something.' Sandy hid his smile. He had a serious message to get across. 'I thought you were told, by several of your seniors including myself, not to get involved.'

'That was a bit like telling somebody to land gently just after his parachute failed to open. I was also told not to lose touch with him. I got the Range Rover stuck and he must have turned back when he saw or heard you ahead of him and he had already fired at me and hit me before I shot him. I fired first, but at his tyre and I missed it.'

This, Sandy decided, would not be a good moment for exploring the ramifications. 'You'll have to face an enquiry, but two superintendents and a chief super have all said that they'll speak up for you – and one of them wasn't even there – so you don't have to worry too much about it.'

Honey raised a hand and made a weak gesture. 'I wasn't worrying. If I wasn't supposed to fire on a known killer who was firing at me, why was I trained to use a handgun? To be honest, I'm more concerned about the Range Rover.'

'No significant damage. One of the chassis members took most of the impact. It'll be out of dock long before you are.'

'That's good.' Her voice sank to a mumble. She relaxed and seemed to doze for a few seconds. When she roused again, she frowned. 'I'm beginning to ache,' she said.

'Didn't they give you an "on demand" painkiller?'

'Somebody said something but I wasn't taking it in.'

Sandy traced a line from a catheter in her wrist to a dangling bag of clear liquid and found what he could only think of as a high-tech bell push. 'Here you are,' he said. 'I had one of these when I was hospitalized in the States. Try not to overuse it.'

'Don't worry. Listen,' she said. 'Keep me posted. I still want first crack at interrogating him. I think I know how to get him going.'

Sandy felt his eyebrows going up of their own accord. 'I don't know what the bosses will say about that.'

'Point out to them that Walsh and I have something in common,' Honey said. 'We shot each other. That forms a bond.'

Sandy tried not to let her see his amusement. 'Try not to form any more bonds that way,' he said. 'I've been worried sick. I thought I was going to lose you and I could not have faced that.'

She reached out and touched his hand. 'Don't blow your nose on the curtains,' she said. That was her usual and unanswerable response to being told not to do something that she had no intention of doing.

The approach of a skein of medical staff interrupted their feast of reason. Sandy was forced to depart but he took with him a list of essentials that Honey wanted to have with her. These included several books that she had acquired but never got around to reading, prints of all the photographs on the digital memory card, her laptop computer and a complete selection of her make-up. Back at the office, Sandy set about a revision of all the documents in the case. Honey, whose recall was generally acknowledged to be phenomenal verging on total, was doing much the same, from memory, as her alertness made a return.

In the days that followed, things moved forward on a dozen fronts. Honey's shoulder began to mend and she came off high dependency and was moved into a private room, by courtesy of BUPA, but at the insistence of several very senior policemen. Answers to the enquiries, few of them significant in themselves but each contributing some fragment to the overall picture, began to trickle back.

And Dougal Walsh was said to be out of danger. He was, said the consultant, strong enough to withstand questioning but unlikely to be very talkative. Honey's demand that she should have the first go at him had been considered and accepted. She made it clear that her interrogation of him would be in several stages.

Honey had been allowed out of bed for an hour at a time for the past two days and felt quite able to walk, slowly, as far as the lifts; but medical staff use wheelchairs as a sort of tagging system. A patient in a wheelchair can be tracked whereas a pedestrian could be anywhere. So into a wheelchair she went despite her protests.

A porter with a brown coat and a mis-placed belief in his own wit trundled her along seemingly endless corridors until she had to agree that the wheelchair was after all a necessity.

Dougal Walsh was still in a high dependency room. He had it to himself for security as much as for any medical reason. A very young-looking uniformed constable with gold-rimmed glasses and a loose mackintosh was in attendance but immersed in a thick book.

The porter parked the wheelchair, advised Honey to speak to a nurse as soon as she wished to be wheeled back to her own ward, and left. The constable had evidently been advised of his duties because he had already produced his notebook and a ballpoint pen.

Honey nodded to him. He triggered a small tape recorder in his top pocket and dangled the microphone beside the bed.

Walsh, it seemed, no longer needed constant medical supervision, but he was surrounded by all the paraphernalia of electronic support and monitoring. His face had not regained its colour and would have looked white except for the contrast with the white sheets and pillows. A bag on a stand dripped something into a vein and most of his bodily functions were being recorded. His heartbeat was producing a regular beep from a monitor. The bedclothes over his right leg were raised over a cage that she thought was probably there to protect the exhaust burn. He looked, Honey thought, distinctly second-hand. She had managed to dress her hair with the help of one of the nurses and she had applied a little make-up on the assumption that any gesture in the direction of femininity might help to intimidate him. Her own face, she knew, had wasted and she had not been to a hairdresser for a fortnight, but Sandy had assured her that she would pass.

Walsh raised his head on her arrival. She wheeled the wheelchair closer to the head of the bed so that they could make eye contact without strain. For immediate support she depended on the young constable. The tape would be listened to and agonised over by her seniors but that would be at a later date, too late to offer immediate advice.

Later, she might have to play the bully, but for the moment a friendly approach was worth trying. 'How are you feeling?' she asked.

'Bloody sore,' he said, without malice. 'What d'you think?' Then he brought his eyes into focus. 'Are you part of my occupational therapy?'

She pretended to laugh. 'You should be so lucky.'

She saw recognition dawn. 'Hey! You're the bitch that shot me.'

'You shot me too.'

'You fired first.'

'At your front wheel. You hit me first.'

'You don't look much hurt.'

'Is it my fault that I'm a better shot than you are?' She decided to terminate the childish exchange. It was time to stir him up. 'Shooting at a police officer is a serious offence. Even possessing a handgun usually merits what they call a custodial sentence. The jail, to you.'

'I meant to shoot past you. I hit you accidentally.' He was lying and she could see it but a jury might believe him.

'How are your thumbs?' she asked.

With an effort he raised his left hand. The

thumb was bandaged. 'Bloody sore,' he said.

'That's just one of the things I have against a semi-auto.' She was feeling her way, hoping that a common interest in the technology of death might open a window. But there was not the least flicker of interest. It looked as though he might relapse again into torpor. She decided to stir him up again. 'How could you bring yourself to kill the girl while you were making love to her?' she asked sharply. 'Are you that kind of a pervert?'

Dougal Walsh jerked in his bed and then groaned. 'For Christ's sake, no,' he said shrilly. 'There was nane o' that in it at all. If things had been different we'd have set up together. Maybe even wanes...'

She produced a scornful laugh. 'Come off it,' she said. 'What kind of love shows itself by killing?'

'You dinnae understand,' he said. For the first time, she could hear desperation and misery in his voice. 'There wis nae future fer us. I kent that. I tried to steer her off frae falling for me. What she kent wis only a wee bit o' the game, but it would hae been enough to start them going along roads tae lead them deeper and deeper. I was telt tae take her away an keep her safe while they asked fer orders. I could see fer myself what the choices were. Either she was bought off or she was killed. I hoped like hell that they'd decide to buy her off. I think a' could have kept her in line.'

'But they decided that the girl had to die? And you were to do the deed?'

'Yes.' His voice sank to a whisper. 'She had to die. You dinnae say no them buggers, the bosses.'

'What buggers?'

'*The* men. The top brass. I thought we might run away together, but how could we hide wi oor faces marked the way they are?'

'Did you tell her that you were going to kill her?'

'No. But I think she kent. She just didnae want me to put ma heid on the block for her. And – kin you no understaund this? – I wanted her to die at her happiest ever. She was worth that. Loving and giving.'

'That's true,' Honey said. 'I may as well tell you that she guessed that her life was in danger, even from you, so she left two letters. And yes, she bears you out. She didn't want you to sacrifice yourself – her self-esteem wasn't strong enough for that. She was prepared to accept whatever came. What on earth induced you to photograph her body and then drop the memory card into a postbox?'

His mouth opened in surprise. 'Is that what became of it? I photoed her so they could see I'd done the job. But I wisna gaun tae hump the camera around wi' me wi' that in it, nor the rude stuff either.' He flushed. Honey was amused to see such modesty in a Glasgow hard man.

'How did it get into the post?' she asked.

'I got the wee camera as part o' a deal wi' Duggie Briar and I fancied it so I kept it until I got word that it was really hot. I bought a new card for it. I had a mate o' mine who kens aboot cameras tae show me how tae swap the cards. When I got home I found I didn't hae the card. I must a left it or dropped it in the pub. Jem Tanar had lifted the camera first and when he kent I was desperate aboot the card he tried to put the black on me, makin out he kent mair than he did, so I stuck him. I'd been back tae look fer it in the pub but there wis nae sign. Some bugger must a found it, seen the postcode on it and drapped it into the postbox. Is that how you tracked me to Haddington?'

'I have the same postcode so it came to me. I must say that I'm surprised at a man like you, knuckling down to a few Glasgow hoodlums.'

The result was all that she'd hoped for. 'A few Glasgow hoodlums, did you say?' He tried to sit up but the effort was too much. All the same, there was a spark in his eye. 'I'll tell you something, Mrs Fancy-Pants. The auld days are coming back. What they call organized crime. It's like it used to be. The gangs are being organized. There's somebody planning what's going down and drawing the skills from all over and, that way, they can tackle bigger capers that ever before. They can call on all the skills they need. Muscle like me. Safe-crackers. Burglars. Forgers. Right up the ladder. That means they can afford to pay off everybody all the way up tae God.'

'And who is this high hoodlum?' she asked. 'The big boss who's doing the organizing?'

He shook his head although she judged that the movement was painful. 'No way!' he said. 'I've told you too much already.' He pinched his mouth shut and turned his head away.

She had got enough for the moment. He had started to talk and he would talk more once he had settled down. If she pushed him, reminded him that he had been ordered by his bosses to kill the love of his life, his change of attitude would be unpredictable. But his attitude might be improved if he had something to worry about. She looked at the young constable. 'Stay alert,' she said. 'Somebody will certainly prefer him dead. Pass the word along.'

'Those are the orders already, ma'am.'

She could see a change in Walsh's eyes. The message would sink in – if he cared whether he lived or died, which was far from certain. She decided to set him off along the path of helpfulness. 'All right,' she said to him. 'Now, do me a favour. Use your bell to call a nurse. I'm ready to go back to bed.'

Twenty-Two

Honey's strength and concentration were making a slow return, but the stress entailed in a change of scene and the concentration of trying to out-think Dougal Walsh had taken it out of her. She dozed and slept and dozed again. It was mid-morning of the next day before she was dragged into full wakefulness, first by the arrival of Constable Knickers with extra chairs, then by a man who she recognized as a police technician, who swept the room for listening devices without finding any such thing, and finally by visitors. It seemed to have been decided that the next meeting of the team leaders was to take place in her hospital room, although if anybody had mentioned it to her it must have been during one of her periods of torpor and had passed her by. If she had been fully awake, she might have been alerted by the presence of somebody, who she later identified as Sandy, who tenderly, if unskilfully, raised her and brushed her hair into some sort of order before laying her down again.

So it was that one detective inspector was caught at a serious disadvantage by two detective superintendents, one detective chief superintendent, one detective chief inspector (her husband) and a constable with notebook and tape recorder. The men seated themselves around the bed so that she was the focus of attention. This might have pleased her on some other occasion, but Honey was caught out in a thin and very short nightdress in which she was not even prepared to sit up to put on her dressing gown. She pulled the duvet up to her chin and remained prone.

Mr Halliday was tacitly recognized as chairman by virtue of his seniority. He addressed his remarks to Honey, seeming quite unperturbed that his only view of her was straight up her nostrils. 'We have all listened to copies and received transcripts of your interview with Dougal Walsh,' he said. 'You were quite right to break off when you did. Give him a day or two to consider his position and he'll come to see that the most he can hope for is to take up the offer that you made him. You agree?'

'Sir,' Honey said, 'I hope so.'

'But you have doubts?'

'I have. He doesn't care much whether he lives or dies. On the other hand, his hatred of the men who forced him to kill his girl is such that he may decide to do them as much damage as he can.'

'I hope you're right. We'll move on and share any progress that we've made.'

'Sir,' said Honey. 'May I say something?'

'Wait your turn, inspector. Mr Largs?'

Detective Superintendent Largs stirred in his chair. 'I have little to report on behalf of Northern. Our one small success has been to identify the man who rented the cottage on the Beauly Firth. He is a resident of Dingwall, by the name of Wyper.' Honey opened her mouth but closed it again. 'He maintains that he rented the cottage for his own occupation, planning a birdwatching holiday, but that family business prevented him from getting away. The man and the girl must have been squatters, he says. Until we can prove him a liar, that doesn't get us very far.

'The lady with the spaniels had been interviewed. She agrees that she posted an envelope for Cheryl Abernethy. The girl, she says, seemed relaxed and happy.'

Mr Halliday nodded. 'As you say, it doesn't take us very far. Mr Blackhouse?'

'Our only success to date has been the capture of Dougal Walsh,' Mr Blackhouse said. 'If Mrs Laird can get him to open up...'

'We'll come back to that subject,' Mr Halliday said.

Mr Blackhouse made a small gesture of acceptance. 'Chief Inspector Laird can report.'

Sandy leaned forward. 'We still have no useful information from any of the planning authorities. Quite probably there have been no formal approaches yet, just concentrated lobbying of the most influential councillors and planning officials and the election of a biddable MSP.

'Dougal Walsh's prostitute girlfriend, Holly Benson, is proving quite willing to talk, but she knows very little and understands almost nothing. It's a matter of keeping her talking and trying to fit together the little bits that emerge. From this, we are putting together a picture of his recent absences, how long he was gone for each time and by what transport. Quite useless at the moment, of course, but almost certain to slot into place before any cases come to court.

'The only other area of progress concerns credit cards. Northern discovered that Walsh had paid for petrol using a credit card issued to a fictitious name at an address care of a post office. As you know, threats have been made against my family and myself. A man who was caught spying on my father-in-law's house, where our child is staying, was searched and he was carrying an identical credit card. Strathclyde think that it may be traceable to Ravitski.'

Mr Halliday's face, unusually, showed expressions of pleasure and surprise. 'If that comes off...' he began.

A young nurse, armed with the confidence that sprang from several months of bossing patients around, came into the room and, ignoring the visitors, began to arrange the materials for the changing of Honey's dressing on a trolley. She soon became aware of the glares of four pairs of male eyes. 'What?' she demanded.

Detective Superintendent Blackhouse told her where to go and how. She flounced out of the room saying something about 'in all her born days...' Her voice faded away along the corridor.

'If that comes off,' Mr Halliday repeated, 'it could represent a good step forward, linking a known killer with Ravitski. That side of the business is becoming urgent. Ravitski's organization of the Glasgow underworld seems to be passing from the planning into the implementing stage. There has been a major robbery from a Carlisle jeweller and a safe-blowing in a mansion house near Newcastle. There was also an attempted bullion snatch at Glasgow Airport, only foiled by luck. Each of those events was well researched and brilliantly planned. No evidence was left behind and nobody talked; the only connection to Ravitski being that the absolute minimum of words were spoken but that any such words were in a recognizable Glasgow accent. Eventually, of course, somebody will become overconfident and we'll have arrests and a show trial, by which time Ravitski will probably be in South America or the Seychelles, laughing at us. So I want this stopped before it gathers momentum. If anybody can suggest any lines of enquiry that we are not already pursuing...?' He began to gather his few papers together.

Honey broke the little silence that followed. 'May I speak now?' she enquired.

For a second time, Mr Halliday's face showed emotion, this time of chagrin. 'I apologize, inspector,' he said. 'I promised you a chance to speak and you've earned it. What can you tell us?'

'Thank you,' Honey said. 'While taking note of your embargo on outside communications, I asked my father to find out something for me. He can be very discreet.'

Mr Blackhouse looked up from the pattern he was making with instruments on the trolley. Honey had already decided that those instruments must be sterilized again before she would allow anybody near her with one of them. 'Robin Potterton-Phipps,' he said.

For an unprecedented third time, Mr Halliday showed an expression, this time combining surprise with respect. 'The industrialist?'

'He has sources of information in the business community,' Honey explained. 'I have found him useful in the past. I asked him to find out for me the names of the man or men behind the *Edinburgh Piper*. He sent me a note that my husband brought me when he visited me yesterday evening. It contains only two names. I had heard the names before but know nothing about their owners. Garth Rigby and Malcolm Wyper.'

Mr Blackhouse started. He dropped a pair of scissors on the floor, but quickly bent to pick it up and return it to a kidney dish. 'Those two!' he exclaimed. 'Men of finance, which position seems to give them the idea that the police are their personal servants. Wyper has one of those huge houses in Ravelstone Dykes and entertains in a big way. Rigby lives out near Kirknewton. To look at, you'd think that Wyper was the country gent – hairy tweeds and heavy shoes – while Rigby, who looks like a professor, with his horn-rims, lives in the country. They're a pair of born complainers and some idiot gave them my name. One dab of graffiti or a thrown snowball and they're on my doorstep demanding a purge. They've been a thorn in my flesh for years.'

'If we're all in luck, you may have a chance

to return the thorn where it belongs. Now,' said Mr Halliday, 'if that's all...?'

'Another thing, sir,' Honey said. 'Were we to understand that the cottage near Beauly was rented in the name of Wyper?'

'You're absolutely right,' Mr Halliday said. 'Let's see if we can trace a connection between Mr Wyper of Dingwall and Mr Wyper of Ravelstone Dykes. The answer may lie in birth certificates, so it's one for Edinburgh.'

'We'll take it on,' said Mr Blackhouse. He looked meaningfully at Sandy.

'Now,' said Mr Halliday, 'are we finished?'

'I don't think so,' Honey said. 'May I please be told what Ravitski looks like? We have at least a description?'

'More than that,' Halliday said. 'I questioned him myself, the last time he was pulled in. He's hollow-chested, rather small, with black hair slicked back, dark eyes and pointed features.'

'Does anybody have a complete set of the photographs from the camera? I mean the whole lot, not just those of the girl.' Sandy fished in his briefcase, produced a large envelope. From it, Honey removed one of four smaller envelopes and pored through the prints until she found one in particular. 'I wondered why Walsh chose to take Edinburgh street scenes. Perhaps he was just familiarizing himself with the camera. But when Mr Blackhouse described the two men of finance, I remembered.'

Halliday took one look. 'Ravitski,' he said. 'And with him...?' He handed the photograph to Blackhouse.

'If that's Ravitski waiting at the crossing,' Blackhouse said, 'the man with him is unmistakably Wyper, complete with ginger moustache. About two paces behind them, the other man looks like Rigby. The photograph's very sharp, it would enlarge many times without losing definition.'

'Now we really are getting somewhere,' Halliday said. 'The three are walking together, there's not a doubt about it. But if we challenge them now, they could write it off as coincidence. Lock it away in the safe. Prosecuting counsel can make great hay with it, after Ravitski has denied knowing Wyper and Rigby and vice versa.'

Mr Largs stirred. 'You'll have to have a care,' he said. 'You may not be allowed to introduce evidence that you haven't intimated to the defence before the trial.'

Mr Halliday surprised them all with a cheerful grin. 'We can introduce it in cross-examination,' he said, 'after they've denied it.'

Twenty-Three

Even for a patient in hospital, there were occasional intervals of peace when nobody wanted to wash her, feed her, bandage her, manipulate her joints or ask an endless series of apparently pointless questions. During those intervals, Honey closed her eyes and tested a series of possible scenarios for her next encounter with Dougal Walsh. She concluded that it was time to play on his fear of women. Femininity seemed to be a doubtful gambit. Perhaps a woman in uniform would bring together his various phobias. Happily she had already asked Sandy to bring in a complete uniform. The hospital's telephone system was overloaded and the use of mobile phones seemed to be considered on a par with patent medicines and back-street abortion. Thinking ahead was an absolute necessity.

However, an enquiry of the medical staff disclosed that Walsh was back on the operating table, which at least postponed the mammoth task of changing into uniform with one arm useless. Two days later the task had to be faced, despite the objections of the nursing staff in whose view the proper day-dress for a patient was nightwear. She managed to bully the youngest nurse into helping with the most difficult adjustments, dressed her hair and made up as best she could one-handed and then demanded the service of a porter with a wheelchair.

To be seen arriving by wheelchair would have lessened her authority; she walked the last few yards, rather unsteadily, and caught the ward sister at the nurse's station. The sister pursed her lips, but a police inspector in uniform, even with one arm in a sling, seemed, in her mind, to override medical confidentiality. Honey received a detailed update on the patient's condition.

She found Walsh reclining palely in the same bed, connected to much the same drips and monitors as on her previous visit. He seemed to have rather more bandages than before. She pulled up a chair and stowed the carrier bag that she had brought with her. There was a basket of fruit on the bedside locker. 'How did that get here?' she asked the bodyguard.

'A visitor came for him.' The man smiled suddenly. 'He didn't get the visitor but we thought that he might as well have the fruit. He doesn't seem to fancy it very much.'

'I can't say that I'm surprised.' She asked Walsh how he was getting on.

'No' well,' he said plaintively. 'No' well at all. They tell me I'll never walk again.'

It was a blatant appeal for sympathy. The bodyguard with the tape recorder and notebook looked up and winked. This time it was an older and more thickset man, one who Honey had not previously met. His bulk made the small room seem more claustrophobic than before. He was sweating slightly in the hospital heating and wearing a loose mackintosh.

Honey blessed the foresight that had prompted her to make her own enquiry. 'That's balls and you know it,' she said briskly. 'They thought at first that I'd clipped your spine but my bullet broke up and only a fragment touched your spine. Any bits that they haven't got out now, they plan to leave. They'll monitor them once every six months to be sure that they're not moving into a more dangerous position.'

'Hey!' Walsh said. 'I didn't even ken that.'

'But you're only the patient,' Honey explained. 'You'll be walking again in a few weeks and running from the police in a year.'

He deflated visibly. 'Why did you ask, if you already knew?'

'I wondered what you'd say and I wanted you to see that we often know more than you

271

think. We usually learn more from what people hold back than from what they say. And thank you for your kind enquiry but my shoulder hurts like hell and they think they'll have to operate again.'

'Well, that's tough,' he said. 'So I'm not such a bad shot after all.' He still was not meeting her eye.

'I still hit you almost dead centre and you nearly missed me. If you're in any doubt we'll have a competition some time, whenever you can manage to remain at liberty for long enough.'

He seemed to brighten. 'You mean, a duel like?'

'No, I do not mean a duel. I mean a target competition on the range.'

'That's no' fair. You've been taught.' He looked directly at her for the first time. 'I'll face up to you wi' a shive any time.'

That, Honey thought, would be the day. 'I should warn you that I've had training in hand-to-hand combat as well. Tell me, why do you suppose this gentleman, or another of the same kind, is babysitting you?'

Walsh shrugged. 'In case I talk?'

Honey looked at the bodyguard. 'Tell him.'

The constable opened his coat and let Walsh see that he had a holster, a truncheon and other items of police weaponry about his person. 'I'm on loan from Strathclyde,' he said, 'because I'd know most of the Glasgow hard men. You had a visitor yesterday afternoon while you were still asleep. Black hair but his stubble coming in ginger. Big ears and crooked teeth. Who does that suggest?'

'I wouldn't know.'

'The name Sullivan Gibbs doesn't ring a bell?'

Walsh swallowed. 'No,' he said hoarsely.

'Too bad. He knew yours all right. As it happens, we already wanted him for killing a tart in Cowcaddens, so we've got him tucked away. But he was after you all right.'

Walsh had lost what little colour remained after his surgery. He produced a twisted smile. 'Was he bringing me fruit? Or flowers?'

'Flowers might have been suitable. He had a hypodermic syringe hidden in a pocket with a rubber cork on the needle. The contents of the syringe have gone for analysis. We'll let you know when the answer comes back, but it won't come as much of a surprise to you. Just don't expect it to be a cure for your allergies.'

'So there you have it,' Honey said. She let any trace of friendliness fall away and became the tough officer on duty. 'There will be others. It's time that you spoke up. Make it easy for yourself. Tell us who you

273

carried messages to and where.'

Walsh sneered. 'And what do I get in return?'

'I can't get you off, you know that. You're in too deep. You'll have to do time.' Walsh was about to speak but Honey cut him short. 'You know too much and they can't trust you any more. You're going to tell me that they could reach you in Barlinnie or Peterhead and snuff you out like treading on an earwig. But we can look after you. I could arrange for you to do your time a long way away, under another name. You can cook; your girl said so. Kitchen supervisor, then. But if you tried to scarper we'd find you, pop you into Barlinnie and let them know where you are. You needn't shake your head at me, my lad. They made you kill your own girl. How much trust could they show you after that?'

'They know I'm not a squealer,' Walsh said. His voice had sunk to a whisper.

'Anyone can be a squealer if he's pushed hard enough, and they know it,' Honey said. 'You've done what they told you so far, but will that save you? You know too much and you've slipped up.' It was time, she decided, to put some cards on the table. 'We know a lot about the refinery site and we're almost ready to move. When we start pulling in everybody right up to the Member of Parliament, who do you think will get the blame? If they were prepared to have the girl killed for what little she knew, how will they feel about you now?'

The mention of an unspecified politician made him blink. Honey hoped that it was enough. She had very little more ammunition in her locker. There was a long pause. 'I'd been wondering...' he said at last. 'There is tougher men than me waitin tae be called. I dinna care a lot, noo that she's gone. I thought I wid but I dinnae. Stupid, in't it? I thought she had to die so I could live and now she's deid I dinna want tae gang on any more.

'The way I see it, my choices are this way. I'm going to go to the jail anyway. They could probably spread money around and get me out, but I'm no' a big enough fish to be worth it. Cheaper tae pay to hae me nobbled in Peterhead or wherever.'

Honey finished the thought for him. 'But if you talk, you may save yourself. You've been carrying messages. You must know quite enough for us to hit them where it hurts. We can take most of them into custody and the rest will be too busy dashing around and trying to save themselves to be bothered about small fry like you. You must know by now that a grateful police force can do a lot to keep a valuable informant safe. Like I said, we can tuck you away under a different name and a long way away from here. You could go by ambulance to London now, this afternoon. We wouldn't even call you as a witness unless we had to. Just give us what you know and we can root out the rest for ourselves. But if you keep your mouth shut, you go straight into Barlinnie or Saughton, and how long do you think you'll last in there?'

He was silent for more than a minute. Then he licked his lips. 'I'm dry,' he said, 'how's about a coffee?'

'That can be arranged,' Honey said. She opened her carrier bag and produced an enormous thermos flask. 'I had this fetched from my hotel,' Honey said. 'Just so that we can be sure nothing's been added to it. I think you may be safe in here for the moment but too many people know that you're here and why. Those are the people who forced you to kill your girl. Now, are you going to talk?'

He met and held her eye. 'No,' he said, 'I'm fucking not. You want to know why? I was brought up Catholic. I believe in an afterlife, whether I wanntae believe it or no'. And if it's true, she's waitin fer me. But if I keep her waiting too long, some other bugger...' He let his head fall back on the pillows.

Honey turned to the bodyguard. 'From

now on,' she said, 'he gets no visitors and no phone calls. He sends out no messages at all. Tell whoever relieves you. I'll have it confirmed through the various channels. Is that the same basket of fruit?'

The constable smiled. 'Sergeant brought another basket up from one of the shops in the entrance hall. The first one went to Forensics.'

'Good. Keep it up. As far as I'm concerned they're welcome to rub out a shit who'd kill his girl while he was seducing her, just to save his own life, but we need him for a little longer.'

'Hey.' Walsh said. 'It wasna like that. I tell-ed you.'

She took a rosy apple and left him to nurse his resentment. It might be a lever to start him talking again.

Twenty-Four

Honey's shoulder remained excruciatingly painful. Physiotherapy brought more pain without improving the condition. Days passed. More detailed X-rays at last revealed a tiny chip of bone that had lodged itself in the joint. She resisted the early attempts to coax her on to the operating table. This was taken to indicate a fear of the surgeon's knife, which in a sense was true. In this age of the hospital superbug, what Honey was terrified of was infection by an imperfectly sterilized instrument or human hand, or even by some virus carried on her own skin. That at least was the excuse she offered both overtly to the staff and subconsciously to herself. In reality, she was in no hurry to escape from the clutches of the hospital. Her baby was safe in Perthshire. As Sandy had reported, one visitor found snooping on Mr Potterton-Phipps's house from a covert had been interrogated and searched. He did not report that, when the man proved unable to explain himself, he had been subjected to a good kicking by the security guards. There was no recurrence.

Sandy went to visit with Minka and his father-in-law at weekends but for the rest of the week he was a faithful visitor. They found the temporary suspension of marital relations tiresome but promised each other an extra-special explosion of loving as soon as it was over.

As days became weeks, Honey caught up with her reading and watched the weather changing over the city and the hills. When the sun shone she wished that she could be out on the hills with Pippa, but in the prevailing weather she was usually content to be in shelter and warmed at the public expense. She remained deaf to the arguments of the doctors, who were anxious to get the bed back and into general use. She managed to exercise secretly while no staff were around.

Honey visited Dougal Walsh every day but he had retreated into a stubborn shell. Most days, he would ignore her presence altogether; but when he did admit to noticing her, he might resort to a sneer or to bad language. Only occasionally would he deign to speak rationally with her, and then only on mundane topics such as the weather or the prospects of Celtic in the Scottish football cup. Honey tried threats, provocation, flattery, lures and tricks but never a word about murder or fraud would he utter. On the subject of his continued incapacitation he was plaintive, barely able to hobble as far as the toilet, or so he said. The medical staff were increasingly concerned.

Honey succumbed at last to the blandishments of her surgeon, a beardless but apparently competent youth with an accent straight out of the Yorkshire Dales. He promised that the operation would be sterile, keyhole and painless, and he lived up to his promises. She had recoiled from allowing him to operate using only a local anaesthetic. The anaesthetist, a tiny Asian lady, promised that Honey would sleep throughout. She realized suddenly that she was being wheeled back to the ward without any perceptible interruption to her conversation with the theatre nurse. It was all over. Her shoulder felt much the same for a day but the pain faded away quickly.

Honey's recovery, however, was kept a strict secret within the hospital, confined to her surgeon, her immediate nursing staff and her physiotherapist. In the presence of Dougal Walsh she put on an act of suffering agonies from her shoulder. The two hypocrites sometimes sneered at each other and sometimes exchanged sympathy.

The three chiefs from the three forces involved continued to meet and to maintain maximum secrecy, but with so little information coming from Honey they had reverted to meeting in Edinburgh. Honey was only kept informed of progress or lack of it by Sandy, who had tired of hotels and moved back into their home. Honey had objected to his living alone where whoever had fired her car could get at him, but by happy chance one of the armed officers who had first occupied the house was temporarily homeless while his bachelor flat was being remodelled and was happy to stay on. There had been no hostile visitors. Sandy began carrying a large bundle of laundry with him whenever he visited his wife's family home, where there were excellent facilities and a laundry maid.

The printing firm remained stubbornly uncooperative and had engaged a senior lawyer to defend the confidentiality of their records and actions. The same lawyer was also representing Geoffrey Manquers MP. The young lady of easy virtue – the only one practising in the area at the time – who had been sharing Dougal Walsh's bed at the time of his arrest had no such representation and was quite willing to talk with a freedom and frankness that one inquisitor said made his hair curl, but she knew very little. She was an occasional visitor to Walsh's cottage. She knew that he was sometimes absent 'on business' but had little idea where he went or what he did when he got there. She knew that the car was not his but appeared mysteriously when he had to make one of his trips. Beyond that, she only knew that after his return from 'up north' he had at first had no use for her services and then had suddenly changed his mind and made furious and frequent use of them.

At last there were signs that the tide was turning in favour of the Law. It is in the nature of crime that the criminal tries very hard to conceal his identity and everything else. Most cases therefore begin in what seems to be a dead end until a breakthrough occurs. Sandy began to bring her news of occasional breaks.

'You remember the girl writing that she used her date of birth as the combination of the wall safe in the cottage? Silly question,' he said quickly, 'you're the original memory maiden.'

Honey would have laughed, but this was before her operation and laughter hurt her shoulder. She managed a grin. 'It's some while since I was a maiden,' she said. 'Otherwise yes, I remember what Cheryl wrote.'

'When they opened the safe – which was behind the wall clock, by the way – there was a watch in it.'

'She also wrote that he gave her a watch,' Honey said.

'Indeed yes. Somebody who knows about watches examined it and it turned out not to be the cheap copy that they'd supposed but a very good original. Following up from the serial number they found that it had been part of the haul from a burglary in Erskine about three years ago. Other items from that burglary were traced to a fence who's a known buddy of Ravitski. There wasn't enough proof to proceed even against the fence, but with Walsh's fingerprints all over it...'

'It all adds up.'

On another visit, Sandy came in shaking raindrops off his waterproofs. He had collected a cup of coffee for himself off a trolley that had not yet reached Honey's room. He gave his wife a kiss in which she could read a disconcerting degree of patience and lowered himself into the rather flimsy armchair. 'What do you remember of the pistol that shot you?' he asked.

Honey thought back for a minute. 'It looked like the Colt Mustang 380,' she said.

'And you say that you don't have a photographic memory! That's exactly what it was. It was one of a batch stolen in transit. It was fired during an attempted – and incompetent – bank hold-up. The culprit was caught. Over the grapevine and off the record, I hear that he was offered Reckless Discharge instead of Attempted Murder if he'd say how the pistol came into his hands. He named Ravitski, who of course denied it absolutely and stuck to his denial. Again, not enough evidence to proceed on but, as you say, it all adds up.'

'So it does. And what else is added to it?'

'That's about it for now. The forensic science lab is still working on our answerphone tape. They've cleaned it up and separated the voice from the background noises. The voiceprint will be good enough to identify the speaker if we ever find him. Among the background noises they have a chiming clock and the voice of a newsvendor which combine to suggest a particular small area of Glasgow. Once again, if we find the man with the voice we may have confirmation.'

The very next day Honey accused Sandy of looking like the cat that got the cream. 'I wouldn't be at all surprised,' Sandy said. 'One brick isn't much on its own, but take enough bricks and put them together and you have a wall. We found a credit card in Walsh's cottage. Before he clammed up, he swore that it must have belonged to the tart who was with him when we came calling. But, as I told the meeting, Mr Largs's men found a filling station where Walsh filled up on the way back south, using that credit card; and the man they caught spying on your father's house had a similar card, on the same account, in his wallet. They're going back through transactions on that account. That should surely lead them back to somebody connected to Ravitski.'

Two days later, he was smiling again. 'We got a recording of Ravitski's voice. The chaps in Forensics are prepared to swear that the voice on our answerphone tape is his.'

These signs that the case was on the move reminded Honey that it was all passing her by. Also, the sun was shining and the glow found its way into a corner of the room. The scene outside could have passed for summer. 'I'm getting nowhere with Walsh,' she said. 'I think it's time that I gave up and came back to work.'

'Work?' Sandy said. 'I've been arguing with Mr Blackhouse that you are still at work. He wanted to count this against your maternity leave and I tried him on adding your time in here as authorized sick leave but he wouldn't wear it.'

'Never mind all that. We'll get our sunshine holiday when this is over. I'm damn sure Walsh is swinging the lead and the hospital wants beds. I suggest that I'll discharge myself and we get them to kick Walsh out unless he speaks up.'

Sandy was nodding. 'Leave it a day or two, I'll talk it over with the chiefs.'

Twenty-Five

There had been an outbreak of a serious flu virus, highly resistant to the inoculations of the previous autumn. The hospital, which was desperately short of beds, discharged Honey with almost indecent haste. She said a less than fond farewell to Dougal Walsh but promised to visit him. He was in a surly mood so she advised him that if he was expecting her to arrive with fruit or flowers he should not hold his breath.

She found the house in reasonable order, considering that it had been in solely male occupancy for many weeks. The guest policeman had returned to his own flat, with apparent reluctance, a fortnight earlier. The Lairds were happy to share the explosion of loving that they had promised. When exhaustion intervened they turned their minds to more practical matters. They packed up the dirty laundry and visited the Potterton-Phipps family home where the laundry facilities were not only superior but were the responsibility of a laundry maid. They found

Minka and June safe and well and apparently contented. Honey's one great fear had been that during her absence in hospital her baby had forgotten her, but she was sure that she could detect signs of recognition from Minka, so it was agreed that June and the baby could remain where they were for a little longer, out of reach of the flu virus.

That this was wise was confirmed by a phone call that arrived shortly after their return home. Honey had refused the offer of a meal out and had rather enjoyed having the use of her own kitchen for a change. When the phone rang they were relaxing, somnolent and replete, in the sitting room. Sandy picked it up but without hurrying. They had adopted the habit of letting the answerphone kick in, so Honey could hear every word.

The same voice with the Glasgow accent and the metallic ring to it spoke. 'You may think that your baby is safe with her granddad but you don't realize how far I'm prepared to go. I have a long arm and you're well within reach. Turn Walsh loose and drop your questions or you'll go back to being a childless couple.' Honey tried to grab the cordless phone but Sandy fended her off. 'And it won't stop there,' the voice finished off.

Despite his own earlier words, Sandy broke

in, 'Mr Ravitski,' he said, 'you are peeing into the wind. Your voice has already been identified by voiceprint and this call is going on to tape. Walsh is free to walk out of the hospital but he prefers it where he is. And I can hardly blame him. He knows that your man Sullivan Gibbs tried to visit him, carrying a syringe loaded with a lethal dose of sodium azide...' Sandy broke off as he found himself speaking to empty air. The phone had gone suddenly dead.

Honey was mentally reviewing the safety factors surrounding Minka. 'Were you not a wee bit rash?' she suggested absently.

'Possibly. But possibly not. I had to disabuse him of any idea that he could get his way by threatening us, because he might have tried to go ahead with his threats. I only told him that his voice had been recognized. He should still know nothing about how far the main investigation has progressed, and if he does know anything he didn't get it from me.'

'I suppose that's true. All right, I'll forgive you.'

'You relieve me. I've been sensing that our trinity of seniors has been feeling impatient. I'm going to suggest that we stir it up a bit.'

Honey considered his words. 'How big is "a bit"?' she enquired.

'As a first step, I suggest that we use this flu

outbreak as an excuse to boot Walsh out into the world, and then keep tabs on him. If he feels both endangered and resentful over the death of his ladylove, the cat may be among the pigeons. And when pussy gets among the dickey-birds, truth comes down among the feathers.'

Honey gave some more thought. 'Well,' she said at last, 'don't put that idea forward as coming from me. If they go for it, you'll be endangering a lot of people. Walsh himself. Any Glasgow heavies that Ravitski sends after him. And, of course, any of our boys that you send on Walsh's tail to guard him.'

'I think you're overstating the case. I've just convinced Ravitski that his identity is known and that he'd be mad to go after Walsh.'

'If he believed you.'

'If he believed me. But I said his name. He'd have to believe me.'

'I am not a passionate admirer of that idea,' Honey said. 'If you want to go ahead with it, give me one more crack at him first. What I suggest is that you tell Walsh that he's being discharged. You take the armed guard off and hide him round the corner where Walsh can't see him. Then, when Walsh feels thoroughly exposed and vulnerable, I'll breeze in on a friendly visit and tell him that there's no danger. That should set warning bells ringing. He'll think it's a trick. This time, my offer of a safe haven in some prison kitchen a long way away may not fall on quite such deaf ears.'

'That,' Sandy said, 'is not bad. I can always trust you to come up with the devious answer. There's just one small snag. I don't care how good a cook he is, I don't like the idea of letting him loose in a kitchen with all those knives around. It might give him ideas about taking a hostage as a first step towards escape. I suggest that you think more along the lines of a library or a laundry.'

'I'll sleep on it,' Honey said.

Sandy waggled his eyebrows at her. 'I'd rather that you slept on me.'

'I can do both,' Honey said happily. 'Golly, is your passion never spent?'

'It was a long time to go without. And in my experience if you let a chance go by, the next opportunity can turn out to be a long way off.'

'I like your thinking,' Honey said. 'Come along.'

Twenty-Six

Two days and much debate went by before the bosses were in agreement to go ahead with the plan. It was the Wednesday morning before Honey got the go-ahead. The main cause of the delay had nothing to do with ethics or risk assessment. It was a matter of the flu.

The outbreak was said to be the most serious since the Asian flu of WWI, if not since the plagues of Egypt. The virus was steadily reducing the numbers of officers available for duty. A successful breakthrough in the cases of corruption over the proposed refinery and of the resurrection of gang culture in Strathclyde might precipitate a sudden demand for officers. The question was whether to try to precipitate and conclude matters before things got worse or to wait for them to get better. The risk that the epidemic might last long enough for the conspirators to make their killing and cover their tracks was the deciding factor. Honey was told to get on with it.

Honey decided to make her first move almost immediately. She drove home, bolted a hasty lunch and changed into uniform complete with radio clipped to her left breast. She had wondered whether something flimsy and clinging might not trigger Walsh's dread of all things feminine, but after consulting Sandy she had decided that the combination of her gender with the authority of the uniform might do the trick again. She paid particular attention to her grooming.

The day had turned bright and sunny – one of those days that assure us, quite wrongly, that spring is here at last. The New Royal Infirmary looked whiter than its usual pale grey against a dark blue sky. She found a parking space not too far from the main doors and hesitated at the shops. But no, to arrive bearing gifts would strike the wrong note.

There was one very noticeable change. Walsh's room seemed strangely uninhabited without an armed guard in evidence. But she had seen a lurking figure near the nurses' station.

If she was reassured, Walsh was not. His first words of greeting were, 'Where's that big gadgie got to?'

Honey took her time seating herself. She placed the usual tape recorder beside the bed and started it recording. 'Your nurse-maid? We decided he'd be more use back on general duty. You're being discharged from hospital in the morning, didn't you know? It's Saughton for you.'

He shook his head. 'When did anybody tell anyone anything around here? Hey, you're throwing me to the wolves?'

Honey sometimes regretted that her nose was not suited to looking down at people and this was just such an occasion. 'The wolves can have you. You're no use to us. You've told us nothing useful. The general feeling is that you don't know anything. You may have been used as an errand boy, but that means very little. If you were sent to so-and-so's house without knowing what was in the message, who cares?'

'Messages are for remembering, not for writing down. I could tell you a whole lot you want to know,' Walsh said. 'If I wanted to.'

'When you want to, give me a bell. I could fix you up with a nice little job. You choose the prison. Anywhere in Britain or Ireland, except a women's prison. We draw the line there.'

Walsh was showing signs of genuine distress. There was sweat on his face and his eyes were staring. 'They can't put me out,' he said weakly. 'I'm still not right. I keep on telling them.'

'And they keep on not believing you.'

There was a long silence. It was evident that Dougal Walsh was thinking very seriously. Honey could guess that he was balancing the risks of becoming an informer against the hope that Ravitski might be sucked down the legal drainpipe, leaving the gang leader with far more to worry about than Walsh and Ravitski's tougher acolytes with no incentive to continue mayhem on his behalf.

Honey decided to press the thought home. 'If you can give us anything to connect Ravitski with the rackets...' she began.

'I could,' he said. 'I surely could.'

'Then do it. Save your own neck. And don't forget that these are the people who forced you to kill your own woman. In your shoes I'd be out for blood.'

For almost the first time ever, he met her eyes. She thought she saw a hot little glow in his. 'Maybe I'm not the vengeful type,' he said. 'You bugger off.'

He turned on his side away from her and she could not get another word out of him.

The figure lurking near the nurses' station turned out to be the young constable who had been on guard during her first visit. He was not quite the invincible powerhouse that Honey had hoped for but when manpower is short you use what you can get. 'Are you armed?' she asked him.

He opened his loose raincoat to show a semi-automatic pistol. 'Just passed the course last month, ma'am,' he said proudly.

The position of the holster had a message for her. 'You're left-handed? If you ever have to fire it in anger, use your right hand to grip your left wrist, not your left hand. That gentleman in the bed there could tell you about the slide. Stay alert.' She left him and walked to the lifts.

Down on the entry level, she visited the shops and sought out a box of Sandy's favourite chocolates. They were June's favourite too, so she made it two boxes. She dropped them on the back seat of the Range Rover and got into the driver's seat. Instead of her radio she used her mobile phone. Within seconds, Sandy was on the line.

Honey had had time to think. 'Sandy, I think I blew it. I was both good cop and bad cop. I gave him the stick and dangled the carrot and I thought for a moment that I had him. Then suddenly he pulled down the shutters. I got something wrong somewhere.'

'You did your best and that's usually pretty damn good.'

'I'd like to think so, but perhaps I made a mistake, reminding him about his girl,' Honey said. 'We'd better think about letting him go with a really good tail on him. If we arrest him just before he moves in for the kill, he may talk and so may his target.'

'And who would you suppose his target would be?'

'That's the interesting bit. Wyper? Rigby? Ravitski? The MP – Manquers, if he's the right one. Ah, yes, that could be very interesting.'

'It would be dangerous but it could open things up. We'd better consult the bosses ... Just a moment, my radio's calling.'

'I can hear it.'

He was back in a few seconds. 'Control wants you but your radio's switched off.'

'I was out of the car and it doesn't work inside the building. Hold on.' She switched on her radio and contacted Control.

Control had an unfamiliar voice and sounded harrassed. 'Oh, Inspector Laird. There's been a call from the New Royal Infirmary. A patient has attacked somebody and absconded. You're the nearest officer, in fact I think you're still at the infirmary, aren't you?'

'I'll investigate. Tell the infirmary to stand by to cut off the lifts when I give the word to the desk. Give me the phone number. And send me some back-up.'

Control read out the phone number. 'Well, I'll try, but...'

Honey had already transferred her attention to the cellphone. 'Sandy, I hope you heard some of that. There's trouble in the New Royal. I think Dougal Walsh has decided not to wait to be discharged into custody. I'm going inside to find out. Can you come and join me? Come to the main entrance and I'll contact you.'

She ran for the doors, ignoring the stares of patients and visitors. Walsh would not have had easy access to his own clothes. At the main desk, a neatly dressed woman seemed to be expecting her and gave her a wave. Honey swung towards her, grabbed a sheet of paper and scribbled her own mobile number. While she wrote, she spoke. 'Has a man gone by? In a hurry, possibly blood-stained, wearing somebody else's coat or hospital overalls?'

'Not that I've seen.'

The New Royal is not a high building. At the lifts, people with sticks and Zimmer frames were standing and grumbling, pushing buttons and asking each other why lifts were always out of service when they were wanted. 'Keep the lifts off until I call you.'

The woman took less than a second to weigh the priorities before shaking her head. 'There could be patients on the way to theatre, haemorrhaging in one of those lifts.'

That was true. Also Walsh might be stuck

in one of those lifts along with two or three nurses. Better to let him go and pick him up again. 'All right,' Honey said. 'Turn the lifts back on. Call me on that number if you see anybody go by who looks like I said.'

The engineers would want to inspect the lifts before restoring service. She could expect several minutes to go by in argument before the lifts resumed. She ran for the stairs. The single flight was a high one. It was soon clear that she was not fully recovered from her long period without real exercise. Her pace slowed as she dragged herself to the first floor; her breath was gasping.

As she neared the floor where Walsh had been nursed, she heard the lifts start again. She ground her teeth and made a horrible face. She would have been as quick and have saved herself a dreadful journey if she had waited for a lift, but few people have that much restraint. She dragged herself up the last few stairs and tried to hurry briskly but with a dignity suiting the constabulary whose uniform she wore.

A nurse was on her knees beside the young constable. She was struggling to stem the flow of blood from a wound in his neck. A stretcher party was emerging from the direction of the restarted lifts. The constable's loose mackintosh was missing, and his shoes. His holster was open and there was no sign of his pistol. The young man looked at her. There was panic in his eyes but he was still in control of himself. 'It wasn't loaded,' he whispered. 'The bugger didn't get any ammo for it.' His eyes closed.

'Did he have a knife?'

'Scalpel.'

Honey's mobile played a disgustingly cheerful little tune – the clog dance from *La Fille mal Gardée*. Reception was poor but she could make it out. 'He just went through the hall,' said the voice.

There was no lift waiting. A quick glance at the indicators did not offer hope of a quick response. Honey whipped out her cellphone again, switched it on and moved until the indicator showed a stronger signal. Sandy answered at the second ring.

'He's away,' she said. 'I'll chase him. Tell somebody to send back-up. I may have made a mistake, reminding him of who gave the orders that caused the death of his girl.'

'I'm sure you're right. He'll try to steal transport and go first for the nearest. That's Malcolm Wyper in Ravelstone Dykes. I'm nearer to him than you are. You head for Kirknewton. Garth Rigby lives just to the south of there, in a very small hamlet called Sullikirk or Sollikirk, it's difficult to read. I gather that his is the only large house. Keep in touch.'

'Will do.'

The lifts still seemed to be responding to calls in the sequence of some programme of their own. Down would be easier than up had been. She gathered up her remaining stamina and headed for the stairs. At least down used a different set of muscles, but taking the stairs three or four at a time gave her innards a jolt every time a foot came down. The effort jumbled her thoughts and when she arrived suddenly in the long entrance hall she had still not oriented her mental map.

She was dashing for the doors when she found her way blocked by a tall but weedy young man in leathers. 'Officer ... I say, officer...' Honey checked. Her errand might be urgent but running over the top of members of the public is frowned upon. 'Officer, my motorbike's been stolen.'

'When and where?'

'From just outside, within the last half hour. I came here to visit...'

Honey was, for the moment, enormously uninterested in which patient he might have been visiting. 'Come with me. We'll follow it up.'

Twenty-Seven

Honey jogged to her car at a pace unsuited to the dignity of her uniform. She could hear the young man thumping along behind her. Dusk was beginning to steal away the daylight. She seemed to be recovering her breath and strength. 'Your bike,' she said over her shoulder. 'It's fast?'

'Very.'

It would be. 'Tank full?'

'Yes.'

Honey scrambled into the Range Rover, opened radio communication and identified herself to Control. 'Leaving NRI,' she said. 'Subject may be heading for Ravelstone Dykes. DCI Laird is on the way there. Or subject may be heading for Kirknewton, which is where I'm going. What about the back-up I asked for?'

'One car was diverted to the infirmary but came on a traffic accident and had to take charge.'

'Then get me somebody else. Divert them to...' The Sat Nav had woken up and

Honey's fingers were working independently. She brought up Kirknewton, identified Garth Rigby's house and read out the coordinates. 'And make it quick.'

'I'll try.'

Honey was ready to scream but with a member of the public sitting beside her she was constrained. She spoke through gritted teeth. 'Do more than try. Succeed.'

'Inspector Laird,' Control said tearfully, 'I am doing my best but this is not my proper job and I've only done it as a holiday stand-in before. Somebody brought the infection first into the control room and it spread from there. Everyone's off with the flu. The supervisor has just given in to it. Mrs Wharton and two other ladies who used to do this job are coming out of retirement to take over and I'm just filling the gap until they get here as best I can but with everybody shouting at me...'

Time was ticking away while she argued with this person. 'Is there anybody else there?'

'Nobody who knows the job any better than I do.'

'Keep trying,' Honey said. 'Subject may be armed and almost certainly intends violence. Broadcast a warning. Divert cars.' She switched off. Sometimes in indignant but otherwise idle moments she had dreamed of reducing Control to tears, but now that she had done so there was little satisfaction in it.

She switched on her cellphone again and pressed it into the hands-free holder. The Range Rover's engine fired at the first touch of the starter. She backed out and pulled into the traffic lane. The young man cleared his throat nervously. 'You don't need me, do you?'

'I do,' Honey said grimly. 'First because you can identify your bike from a distance. Secondly because I may need a witness.' Thirdly, she thought grimly, because I may want somebody to tell my husband that I died bravely, thinking of him.

Happily, she had possessed herself of a blue light that attached to the vehicle's roof magnetically. With this in place and flashing, she was able to carve her way through the traffic. Using her horn instead of a klaxon she thrust and bullied her way. Her mouth was dry but she had to fight her bladder. She sent up a fervent hope that Sandy would catch their quarry at Ravelstone Dykes and then she followed it with a postscript cancelling the first prayer. If somebody were to meet the infuriated Dougal Walsh, especially armed with a scalpel, she would prefer that it was anybody other than Sandy. Even herself.

The suburban sprawl of Edinburgh spreads along the radial roads, the A-70 not least.

The Pentland Hills began to rise on her left. The traffic was patchy but frighteningly dense at times. Now and again she was forced to slow or even to stop, but by thrusting onward she could usually force a quick passage, the vehicles on either side seeming to pull apart, blurred by her speed. As the daylight faded the flashing blue light seemed to gain authority.

They were near the turning for Kirknewton when Sandy came on the phone. 'Too late,' he said. 'Walsh has been and gone.'

'And ... the householder?'

'Don't ask. Walsh left a scalpel here, by the way.'

'Follow me when you can and divert any back-up to follow.'

'Will do. But I have to wait for the first back-up to arrive. I've called for an ambulance.'

'Come when you can,' Honey said. To her passenger she added, 'He'll be coming here, probably on your bike. Watch out for it. What's your name, by the way?'

'I'm Warren Hart.'

'Watch for your bike, Warren, but stay well out of harm's way. I had no business dragging a civilian along with me on an errand like this.'

One comfort was that Dougal Walsh had left his scalpel at Ravelstone Dykes. Probably he had found a knife to replace it. She would rather have faced a battleaxe than a scalpel, but that was probably down to the association of scalpels with sharpness and deep incisions.

Kirknewton was somewhere to their right but, directed by the Sat Nav, she turned left in the direction of the Pentland Regional Park and soon came within sight of Garth Rigby's house. Mr Rigby seemed to fancy the life of a rural laird. His single-storey house did not have the high-windowed proportions of the older Scottish houses but it was spacious and spreading in a site of several landscaped acres set among fields and screened from its nearer neighbours by a small wood.

Honey let her headlights play over the front of the house and then switched them off. There was enough light left in the day to drive by, hoping that any other drivers would be showing lights. Beyond a curve in the road she saw gates on her left and a driveway leading to the front door between what seemed to be lawns dotted with specimen trees. She let the car drift to a halt against the hedge.

'I'll have to go to the house,' she told her companion. 'Do you have a mobile phone?'

'Yes.' He sounded surprised at the question, as if everybody had a cellphone in this day and age.

'Give it to me.' She took it. It was a familiar model. She keyed her own mobile number into it. 'Stay here. If anything develops, particularly if you see your motorbike, call me. OK?'

'Right.'

Honey left the Range Rover, closed the door softly and walked back to the gateway. Her rubber soles made little sound on the tarmac. She turned in at the gateway. Two adjacent windows, presumably of the same room, showed light behind curtains and there was a glow at the front door. She hurried silently over grass. There was a car on the hardstanding. Even in the gathering dusk it was unmistakably a Jaguar. Gravel would have necessitated a detour but the driveway was tarmac.

The front door was recessed and in deep shade. There was a shadow beside the door but Honey was fairly sure that it was not Dougal Walsh. She forced herself to approach and the shadow resolved itself into just that – a shadow. She tried the front door. To her surprise and some disquiet, it opened under her hand. Routine suggested that she should ring the bell, march in and call loudly for the householder, but that would be the best course only with back-up waiting within call. The alternative would have been to wait for help to arrive, but that help seemed to be so remote that she would end up confronting Dougal Walsh anyway – a confrontation that she would prefer not to have in growing darkness. She slipped through the door and closed it very gently behind her, making sure that she knew how to open it in a hurry.

She was in a generous but softly lit hallway, freshly and lavishly decorated with what she knew to be very expensive wallpaper, some sporting prints and a table and two chairs that were either antique or good reproductions. The carpet was of such a quality that she felt that taking off her shoes would be only proper.

A heavy flush door on her left probably lead to the room where she had seen a light. Over the pounding of her heart she could hear voices. She eased down the handle. As the crack opened, she could hear that one voice seemed to be raised in fear. The other was low, and from the cadence she thought that it was that of Walsh.

She let the door open wide enough for her to slip through. The hinges were oiled and silent.

The scene opened up as suddenly as a film clip. Honey gained an immediate overall impression, but several seconds passed while she absorbed the macabre details. Almost at her feet lay a plump woman in a dressing gown, either unconscious or dead. There was blood on her face and purple bruising was showing on her jaw. Dougal Walsh was standing in the middle of the room, leaning painfully against a chair back. Honey recognized his Glasgow tones and glottal stops. His right hand held a kitchen knife with a blade the length of a hand's span. It was bloodied and it looked sharp.

Facing Walsh and Honey was a man who had to be Garth Rigby. From his name and other attributes, Honey had expected him to be a beefy, red-faced countryman. Instead, Rigby turned out to be a slim man of academic appearance, almost bald and, to judge by the broken spectacles on the floor, not well gifted with eyesight. The only sign of a rustic habit was the suit of checked tweed plus twos that he wore with heavy brogues. He was seated in a high-backed chair. His hands appeared to be tied together behind the chair. Numerous cuts and jabs, still leaking blood, combined to explain how he had come to knuckle down and accept domination and bonds.

He still had his wits about him, however. He recognized Honey's entry into the room but he had enough command of himself to avoid, after one startled glance, betraying her presence. He fixed his eyes on Walsh's and held the other's gaze. His jaw was clamped shut, which might have been taken for reaction to the pain of his wounds but which Honey thought was stubbornness.

'You bugger!' Walsh said. 'It was on your orders I had to kill the girl, yours and Wyper's, and I've just given him what he had coming. It's your turn next but I'll make you suffer first. What do you say to that?'

Honey was in no doubt that whatever Rigby said would only trigger further violence. The man must also have sensed it. He stayed silent. Honey was moving silently forward. In her mind she was reviewing what she had been taught about disarming a man with a knife. A lesson in a gymnasium with a wooden knife was a far cry from a luxurious room and a furious killer with a knife that looked larger and sharper every moment.

She had only taken two silent paces when the phone in her pocket began to play its jolly little tune. Walsh span round, aiming his knife at her torso in a way that made her want to cringe. He backed towards his prisoner.

For years, Honey had been habituated to react to the ring of a mobile phone. Without conscious effort she found the phone in her hand. 'My bike's in the hedge,' said Warren Hart's voice.

'He's here,' Honey said. It seemed to be the only message worth passing. She snapped the phone shut and dropped it into her pocket.

Walsh was standing beside Rigby, the knife at Rigby's throat. 'Stay where you are while I finish the business,' he said. 'Then I'll come for you. After that, I'll finish myself. She'll be waiting for me.' He moved the knife and made a long cut in Rigby's face.

'You were going to face me,' Honey said. She forced a smile. 'We both know that I shot better than you did and you promised to face me with a knife. Well, now's your one chance.'

Walsh froze. Undecided, he was considering whether to kill Rigby first or to save him for afterwards. 'What's the matter?' Honey asked him. Her voice had become very husky and she had to fight to prevent it going up into a squeak. 'Are you afraid of one woman? I don't even have a knife. I'm here. Come and get me.'

Walsh pushed Rigby's head away and walked unsteadily towards her, the knife leading him. 'Let's see if you're as good as you think you are,' he said. He stumbled forward a pace and then ran at her.

Honey crossed her hands, palms down, applying the cross-arm block just as she had been taught at Hendon. Those hours in the gymnasium had not been wasted. She had him in an armlock but he did not drop the knife. She turned the lock into a judo hold and threw him. He was facing her and their eyes were locked. He had fallen on the knife, which protruded from his abdomen. Their eyes were locked. 'You're good,' he said hoarsely.

She heard the klaxons of the promised back-up.

Twenty-Eight

Garth Rigby and Mrs Rigby survived, concussed and scarred but not seriously injured. Malcolm Wyper was more badly damaged but due largely to Sandy's early arrival, he too survived.

When Dougal Walsh fell on to his own knife (or, to be more precise, the knife that he had purloined from Malcolm Wyper's house) the knife had turned sideways so that Walsh lost a lot of blood but no major organs were damaged. His violent exercise, however, had partially undone the good work that the surgeons had performed on him after the shooting. After a lengthy period in surgery he was declared out of danger. He was put under permanent suicide watch, but by now his emotions had become focussed on his hatred for those who had forced him to kill Cheryl Abernethy. Prevented from further physical attacks, he made and signed a long statement. He had been the principal messenger between Ravitski, all the conspirators and the Glasgow gang leaders whom

Ravitski had been in the process of welding into a nucleus of organized crime. It was said that Chief Superintendent Halliday went singing about the office for a whole day.

Part of Walsh's resentment was reserved for Honey, who he regarded as having been his nemesis throughout. Through a solicitor provided by Legal Aid, he argued that Detective Inspector Laird had first shot him and then, later, tried to stab him fatally. This resulted in a suspension, which Honey spent with Sandy and Minka in one of the family's Mediterranean timeshares, and a hearing at which she was supported not only by two superintendents and a chief superintendent but also by Garth Rigby. Mr Rigby, while not admitting to one word of what Dougal Walsh was alleging about him, was out-spoken in his admiration for Honey's courage in facing down an armed killer. The media had a field day.

Dougal Walsh was later found hanged in his cell.

The disappearance of Mr McRitchie was never satisfactorily explained. Honey was left to wonder whether he had been an in-nocent whose involvement with Cheryl had sealed his fate or an accomplice who had been spirited out of harm's way. The ques-tion was put to Ravitski at his trial but he denied all knowledge of the journalist.

Honey's name was put forward for a Queen's Medal. The media again made a meal of it.

The glow surrounding her was only a little tarnished in the eyes of Mr Blackhouse when she pointed out to him that she had had some sick leave and a period of suspension on pay but that she had still not taken the maternity leave to which she was entitled and which he had agreed in writing to defer.

During the period while the media were reporting the pursuit, the confrontation, the arrest, Walsh's trial and Honey's hearing, Kate Ingliston had kept her head down and her profile low. Later, she admitted to a feeling that any mention of the memory card might bring the card and its contents to the attention of the lawyers, the media and the waiting world. When the tumult and shouting were beginning to die down, an enterprising journalist decided that there would be a book in the twin subjects of the oil refinery (which by then was under construction but on a different site) and the attempted resurgence of organized gang culture in Glasgow.

Honey had assured Kate many times that the memory card was safely destroyed, but Kate returned to the subject once too often. 'And there are no copies?' she demanded.

'I've told you and told you,' Honey said.

'There are copies in police files, in legal files, in computers, in media libraries, but none with your faces to be seen. Most of the copies that found their way into the papers and on to the TV screens were oblique shots of prints held in people's hands.'

'So there's no risk of this writer getting his hands on any copies with my face on them?'

Honey's patience was at last exhausted. 'No. But you'd better keep your knickers on in the future,' she said. 'That bum of yours is unmistakable.'

Kate gasped. 'In what way?'

'If you don't know, I'm not going to tell you.'

Kate dashed home where she was discovered by her husband, making unconventional use of several mirrors.